The BAFFLER

NUMBER ELEVEN

Thomas Frank, editor-in-chief • Greg Lane, publisher
"Diamonds" Dave Mulcahey, managing editor
Matt Weiland, editor-at-large
Damon Krukowski, Jennifer Moxley, poetry
Keith White, senior editor
Kim Phillips-Fein, Tom Vanderbilt, Chris Lehmann
contributing editors
Lisa Haney, cover • Greg "Martin" Martin, traffic
George Hodak, Jim McNeill, hodaktors

THE BAFFLER wishes to thank Doug Henwood for the epigraph-graph and accompanying text, both of which originally appeared in *Left Business Observer*, and Seth Sanders, publisher of *A Nest of Ninnies*, for coordinating "Cordon Sanitaire."

A special thanks to Bill Ayers, Bernardine Dohrn, Frank Rich, John Ayers, Tom Geogheghan, Gretel Braidwood, and Brad Kotler and his esteemed colleagues.

Thanks also to all the bookstores and individuals we haven't already acknowledged for helping out on the "Business and the American Mind Tour": Brishen Rogers, David Tritelli, Gayle Wald, Sandy Zipp, Bill Serrin, Stacy Leigh, Robert McDonnell, Sharon Jones, Derek Vandermark, the Chicago Department of Cultural Affairs, Matt Bakkom, Michael Dust, Michael Tortorello, Chris Wilcha, Skylight Books, Daily Planet Books, University Press Bookstore in Berkeley, Christian Parenti, Left Bank Books in Seattle, and City Lights Books in San Francisco.

"Saturday Night at the Movies" is reprinted with permission from Dalkey Archive Press from *Memories of My Father Watching TV*, by Curtis White. Copyright © 1998 by Curtis White. The photographs from *The Third Man* were provided by the British Film Institute. The four articles in "I, Faker" originally appeared in The Central New York *Business Journal* and are reprinted with the permission of the publisher.

This BAFFLER was produced by its editors in the summer of 1998, without benefit of focus groups, town-hall meetings, phone polls, beeper studies, or, in fact, any input from the public at all. We call the research method that we use "thinking." We call our journalistic method "writing." For a couple ten thousand in foundation money, though, we'll gladly take up the standard of civic empowerment, start worrying about the problem of media cynicism, and conduct interactive double-blind placebo studies on the Internet.

The editors invite submissions of art, fiction, and essays. All submissions must be accompanied by a stamped, self-addressed envelope. Unsolicited poetry submissions will not be considered.

Please send address changes and everything else to us at the address below.

P.O. Box 378293, Chicago, IL 60637

Triangulation Nation
Affirming Mediocrity in a Jaded Age

Thomas Frank

But there was more than civility on the panel. There was active goodwill. It was clear that we wished one another well. We wished the President well.

—Roger Rosenblatt, describing a 1998 TV appearance in *Time* magazine

Back to Normalcy II: The Theory

UPPER-MIDDLE-CLASS life still has its comforts, to be sure. If anything, the suburban piles are getting bigger, the SUVs more imperious, the hotel employees more servile, and the frequent-flier perks more lavish. But turn on the TV and revolution reigns. The old symbols are burning, the common folk are sneering. The middle class may have its luxuries, but it has lost its chorus of idealizers, the flatterers who once did so much to define American life. From *Sabrina* to *Springer* we're roaring against the suburban way. We want to tell the world our version of *Peyton Place*, our beef with the middle-class horror. The great middle no longer believes, and in the things that once amused it so easily it believes least of all. Its crushing doubt coughs up *South Park* and *The X-Files*, leads us to scoff at classic bits of uplift like the Modern Library's Top One Hundred, and reduces even Gibraltars of middlebrow like *Reader's Digest* to rubble. We are none of us surprised when the blow job is promoted from bathroom graffiti to national emblem, the republic for which it stands a place where interns and content-providers live to do little more than service the vain prerogatives of presidents and celebrities.

For others, though, this cultural moonscape of the always-already muckraked is hardly a happy one. From old right-wing plaints about "heroes" and the lack thereof there has arisen an elaborate new social theory, a dream of "civil society," a middle-class utopia of order and quiet respectfulness. Think tanks convene; foundations grant; op-ed writers solemnify. The deeds and deaths of astronauts, the anniversaries of battles, the syndication of TV shows from a more naive time are all occasions for ruminating on the nature and disappearance of civility.

Nowhere has the weight of public doubt been felt more heavily than in journalism, where the collapse of the old middlebrow formulas has precipitated a nasty legitimacy crisis, a sense of lost authority that has in turn inspired a towering mass of wordy self-examinations and confessions. The news legitimacy crisis can be described in any number of statistical or metaphorical ways, depending on the reporter's requirements: Circulation is declining; Generation X is scoffing; other media are encroaching on the turf of network and newspaper; and journalists themselves are blundering wherever one turns, their negligence further opening the floodgates of public doubt. Then there is the nightmare statistic, that mounting tidal wave of public disgust with the press that is reflected by poll after poll, popularity contests that journalists seem always to lose—whether it's to politicians, salesmen, phone solicitors, TV preachers, dogcatchers, prison guards, Mafia chieftains, computer moguls, second-story men, you name it. Journalists are sensationalists, distorters, and liars, Americans now seem to believe, as universally corrupt and untrustworthy as the elected officials with whom they're supposed to be perpetually at war. Their social position no longer secure, their power to shape public discourse no longer irresistible, and their traditional prerogatives now the right of any drudge who speaks html or knows how to run a photocopier, journalists are in danger of being demoted altogether, of embarking on that long slide from profession back to mere job.

To make matters worse, news-debunking now rivals news-writing as a legitimate occupation, as a booming shadow industry of media columnists, watchdog magazines, radio hosts, online commentators, and freebooting critics set out to undistort the media's distortions for the misinformed masses. The mendacity of the press is so well-understood that it no longer requires any elaboration before being introduced as a plot device in sitcom and film. It has given every city its own media columnist, churning out news stories about news stories that were themselves about news stories. Even advertisements for *Fox News*, possibly the most degraded of news programs, announce that network news has gone too far, but that this network, by God, still believes in the consent of the governed: "We Report. You Decide."

For as long as there has been a fourth estate, journalists have suffered the slings and arrows of public outrage—mob action, duels, dynamite, death squads. But to have their own weapons of skepticism and doubt turned on them . . . that really *hurts*, man. Other industries close to the great middle have discovered ways to manage the collapse of faith—think of the auto industry, which routinely transforms our disgust with its high-handed self into new reasons to buy cars; or magazine writing, locked these days into a sort of arms race of attitude; or advertising, where hip campaigns have for years acknowledged public distrust as a way of distinguishing the claims of one brand from another. Journalists, however, look out at the great statistical monolith of public doubt and see doomsday.

And they are penitent indeed. A burgeoning literature of journalistic autoflagellation proclaims that all this public mistrust is, for once, right on target, that it is journalists' own poisonous "cynicism" that is to blame, that unless this corrosive cynicism is stopped soon, it will destroy nothing less than "the Republic" itself. It is a time of desperation in that Washington-based encampment of hypernormalcy that is the punditocracy, and the commentator class has wheeled in formation to face its tormentors, issuing forth vast reams of journalistic wisdom, diagnoses of the malaise, and schemes by which the middlebrow republic might be redeemed. In one compilation of lamentations, *Feeding Frenzy,* by political scientist Larry Sabato, Beltway journalists assess their "attack-dog" practices and their "adversarial" behavior. Joseph Cappella and Kathleen Hall Jamieson, in *Spiral of Cynicism*, summon up so many Beltwayer confessions of malevolence that the authors' conclusion—journalists have *caused* the dread "cynicism" that stalks the land—seems positively superfluous. It is a staggeringly arrogant notion, this idea of a public mind poisoned by an overdose of journalistic zealotry, and yet so nicely does it flatter the power of a declining profession that it is repeated virtually wherever the press's legitimacy crisis is being discussed.*

To be sure, some worthwhile work has come of these journalistic mea culpas. In *Breaking the News,* veteran editor James Fallows administers a series of much-deserved hidings to the various lights of the Washington press corps. He writes intelligently about the changing class interests of journalists and their consequently skewed perspectives, and capably trashes the pontifications of John McLaughlin, Cokie Roberts, and the redbaiting twister Robert Novak. Jay Rosen, former media critic for *Tikkun* magazine (and, like Fallows, a standard-bearer for the public journalism movement), blasts the tendency to reduce political coverage to tales of one politician's tactical advantages over another in his book *Getting the Connections Right.* Cappella and Jamieson demonstrate that by focusing on the superficial conflicts between Clinton and Gingrich in 1995, the press utterly missed the two men's collusion on larger issues.

---

* Unfortunately, it's also a wrong notion. A 1995 Times Mirror poll found that fully 77 percent of the public rated the honesty and ethics of public officials as low, while only 40 percent of journalists believed the same. If journalists were to faithfully represent the views of the public they serve, as the tenets of public journalism seem to mandate they do, they would have to become *more* cynical, not less.

But having landed these blows, each critic then proceeds to make the same gargantuan error. For all their moaning over "adversarialism," not one of these authors seems to have the faintest idea what the word means. While Bob Woodward, the poster-boy of "attack dog" journalism, may have occasionally put politicians in difficult positions, his writing hardly raises a meaningful challenge to the foundation of American order, to the rule of the market. Nor can any of the other journalists cited in these books be said to regard the exercise of American power as an alienated outsider, or as an opponent of the existing economic order, or even as someone with ideals substantially different from those of the generals and senators and administrators on whom they so obsessively focus. A more fruitful analysis of the intellectual failings of America in the Nineties might begin not with the media's "adversarialism" but with its mountainous *smugness*, its unthinking reverence for free markets and global trade, its unquestioning embrace of the advertised life and its refusal to consider alternatives to the corporate order. It might take into account the industry's trans-Seventies past, its proud and ancient status as a leading pillar of consensus. One might begin by wondering why it is that the United States has the *least* truly adversarial journalism of any Western nation; why it is that ours is the only country where the transparently false bromides of the market encounter only the feeblest of demurrals in the daily press and never a peep of the kind of excoriating refutation to which they are routinely treated in such un-cynical places as Mexico, France, or India; how it came to be that our journalists boast so proudly of their independence when they are closer to the thinking of the elites of industry and government than their counterparts in almost any other land.

Oddly enough, this is exactly where critiques of the press began for figures like Upton Sinclair and George Seldes. Maybe journalism's problems, they reasoned, arise from the forcible application of business principles to an enterprise where business ought to have very little place. Maybe each of our contemporary problems, from the peculiar institution of journalistic "objectivity" to the inability to contextualize to the rise of celebrity pundits, is related to the fact that journalism has been swallowed whole by the culture of money. Maybe the decline of American journalism is one of the most glaring and shameful tales of market failure in our history, an object lesson in a simple fact the molders of middlebrow opinion will not face up to: Corporations do not act on behalf of the public good. (Rosen, to his credit, does admit that such a critique of the press exists and that it is accurate, but then criticizes it for being too "depressing," suggests that it is not "productive" enough, and then turns resolutely away from it.)

Historical context is evidently too much of a leap for contemporary news-thinkers. Almost without fail their books follow the same mysterious trajectory, veering from scathing indictments of pundit idiocy to airy musings about civil society and its virtues. In place of cynicism, it is said, journalists must try hard and dedicate themselves to service. We must have a "public journalism" that, in Jay Rosen's maddeningly vague terms, "clears a space where the public can do its work," which can "engage people as citizens," which will "help revive civic life and improve public dialogue."

It sounds quite noble, this "public journalism." But what, specifically, does it mean to apply democratic principles to the information industry? Were we not so blinded by the language of the market triumphant, the answers would be obvious: Promote local ownership of newspapers somehow, or reduce the power of advertisers, or break up the Culture Trust, or, at the very least, secure decent wages and working conditions for journalists and pressmen. But public journalism is an idea that has achieved prominence through the support of the big foundations—proud towers of middlebrow given to high-minded causes like "empowerment" or "involvement" and bearing names like "Do Something"—and as such it is naturally allergic to considerations of institutional power. Prominent proponents of public journalism like Rosen and Fallows have almost nothing to say about reshaping journalism as an industry, about changing the relations of economic power. What they mean by "democracy" is a kind of *cultural* democracy, a weird populism according to which the root of all the industry's problems is the "elitism" of particular writers, their refusal to "listen" and their tendency to favor expert opinion over that of the people. And the solutions for which the public journalists call—an extensive use of polls, "town hall meetings," and focus groups to ensure that newspaper stories take into account the actual concerns of the public rather than the cynical urges of the self-centered writer—are about as likely to offend journalism's conglomerate parents as would a demand for, say, a more comprehensive astrology column.

And, sure enough, once their anger at the Beltway boobs has passed, the theorists of public journalism indulge their middlebrow tendencies without shame or reservation, returning again and again to the most innocent, even infantile, formulations of democratic theory. Rosen is particularly given to hollow Fifties-era phrases like "the American experiment" and "our lengthy adventure in

I, Faker

Paul Maliszewski

I must confess. I must tell what I have done.

I was a staff writer at *The Business Journal* of Central New York, and my job was less than rewarding. When called upon, I cobbled together special sections on annuities, offered tips on executive gift-giving, and wrote brightly about business prospects in Syracuse—whose economy had been stagnant for the last decade. I was a hack and I knew it. What's more, I had come to see my hackwork as not just flimsy and inconsequential but insidious. One article on a welfare-to-work program was 100 percent free of interviews with any actual workers; the publisher praised it for being balanced. Like Onondaga Lake, located just upwind from where I wrote, my articles not only smelled a little peculiar, they polluted the air around me. They were toxic.

Perhaps I could have endured this job for many more years, but fearing the consequences of my labor, I finally decided that I could no longer look away. I needed somehow to address all the issues the paper consistently ignored. Why, for example, hadn't this journal of business published a single article about the epic, $1.5 billion securities fraud perpetrated by the Syracuse-based Bennett Funding Group—one of the largest Ponzi schemes in history? Why was one of my colleagues writing an editorial about the NAACP, placing at the crux of his analysis the marital history of its current president? While Syracuse burned, the publisher acted as if the civility of the nation depended on the distinction between "who" and "whom," the managing editor practiced calling himself with a cellular phone he received compliments of an advertiser for research purposes, and the other writers debated the merits of "among" vs. "amongst." Disgusted, I wrote a Swiftian letter to my own editor:

The Business Journal, September 1, 1997

To the Editor:

Three cheers and then some for Norm Poltenson's "Ladder Without Rungs" editorial in the August 4 issue of *The Business Journal*. Poltenson points out that the United States, with its dynamic, revolutionary economy, is by far the superior of Europe. . . .

However, earlier this week my American reverie was shattered as I read that the ungrateful workers at UPS have gone on strike. The men (and women) in brown are saying the company hired too many part-time workers and that they are required to lift loads that are too heavy and handle too many packages an hour. Please, I thought. First brush aside these sugary, humanist sentiments, and let's get down to facts. UPS carriers are required to lift packages weighing up to 150 pounds. Sorters are expected to handle 1,600 packages per hour. While I'm not sure I can lift 150 pounds or even count to 1,600 in an hour, the brown people of UPS are, in fact, professional sorters and carriers and naturally suited for this kind of work. It is their job to sort and carry. Moreover, they should cease with their shrill complaints. If the striking brown clowns (workers) should dare seek a more humane corporation, they would do better to seek a good psychotherapist.

To put the complaints of those UPSers in perspective, let's consider the true success of the company. In 1996, UPS made $1 billion in profits. But it hasn't been all up. Since 1990, UPS has paid $4.4 million in penalties for health and safety complaints, for more than

nationhood," and to maudlin descriptions of the perils that beset such high-minded ideas. Fallows seems to believe that national discord is something invented by journalists; that social conflict is alien to American shores; and that if only "elite journalists" would "listen" to the people rather than poison the democratic process with their "adversarialism," the few problems we face would be quickly solved. He speaks heartily of one newspaper's "Public Life Team" ("We will lead the community to discover itself and act on what it has learned") and Rosen hails the "People Project" launched by another, both monikers so grandly meaningless that they could well be brand names for lines of Japanese footwear.

However simplistic, this reduction of journalistic error to questions of personal arrogance, to an unfamiliarity with the ways of the people, strikes a powerful American chord, and by this year "elitism" was rivalling "cynicism" as the free-floating explain-all whenever some explanation is required for journalistic malpractice. From the Stephen Glass episode to the Lewinsky circus, the media "establishment" is said to be arrogant and out of touch, guided by its own ideas rather than those of the citizenry, endlessly "widening the gap," as one hand-wringing *U.S. News* column put it, between their snobbish selves and "the rest of us." As so many other strains of romantic pseudo-populism have done before, public journalism seems to understand critical judgment itself as an arrogant, undemocratic act. "Elitism," that cardinal democratic sin, is a quality that Fallows repeatedly associates with hyperjudgmental figures like Novak and McLaughlin; the error of the "media Establishment" consists of "talk[ing] *at* people rather than with or even to them." "Democracy," meanwhile, is a sort of eternal suspension of judgment, a process of endless "listening," "ambivalence," and virtuous deference to "the popular will." Rosen insists even more forcefully that journalists have no business giving an arrogant thumbs-up or thumbs-down on everything our leaders do, but should instead constantly be wondering about who they are and whether or not they are representing their constituency, the public, and asking the questions that the public would want them to ask. He calls his model of democratic journalism "proactive neutrality," a process of soliciting conversation with the public—"bringing people to the table"—but never "telling them what to decide." Beneath its therapeutic warmth, the obvious implication of such an idea is that democratic culture has no place for crusading or even persuasion; these are by definition acts of cultural "elitism." Another implication is that journalists can save their profession from the certain death of public doubt only by replacing its elitist ideas with the tools of mass marketing. Through the focus group and the telephone survey we can catch a glimpse of The People; only by embracing the democratic devices of big business can we persuade Them to believe again.

It may seem a rather embarrassing intellectual error to look out at the America of 1998, in which more and more aspects of public life are being brought under corporate control, in which the concentration of wealth and the growth of poverty are at record levels, in which no group or figure, public or private, dares challenge the authority of the market, and in which so many aspects of the general welfare are breaking down, and to declare that the problem facing democracy is an excess of judgment. It may seem strange in such circumstances to argue that the answer to such acute and well-defined disorders is to shut up, stop criticizing, and contemplate instead the majesty of The People.

But in fact it is fully in the American grain. Confusing democracy with the suspension of judgment is, like ringing evocations of "the American experiment," a classic element of American middlebrow. It recurs, for example, with striking consistency throughout *One Nation, After All,* sociologist Alan Wolfe's recent survey of upper-middle-class American attitudes. Almost to a man, the American bourgeoisie is evidently convinced that democracy means nobody's views are any righter than anyone else's. "To exclude, to condemn, is to judge," Wolfe writes approvingly, "and middle-class Americans are reluctant to pass judgment on how other people act and think." It is presumptuous to believe too strongly in anything, insists the voice of the great middle, because by so doing we risk visiting bad feelings and exclusion on those who might disagree.

The path to salvation is clear: Journalists must become better democrats by becoming better businessmen,

1,300 violations documented by OSHA. Let us assume, conservatively, that those violations and penalty payments were made in equal amounts over the last seven years. Thus, UPS paid about $630,000 for an average of 186 violations a year. I bring this up not to berate UPS, as *The New York Times* did. Rather, I want to suggest that the penalty (a trifle really for a billion-dollar corporation) is in effect one of the wisest investments it could make. Indeed, in order to continue on its path to success and improve its already considerable profit margins, UPS must act aggressively now and take risks. One way to do this is to make its workplace riskier. To wit: would not UPS at least double its profits by raising the number of its OSHA violations to 372 for 1998? Could it not fairly triple or quadruple its profits by budgeting for and investing penalty amounts of $1.2 million or $1.8 million in fiscal years 1999 and 2000?

By considering my simple proposal, corporations like UPS and others will guarantee that the United States remains a vibrant economic dynamo of a country.

What I need to confess is I didn't sign my name to these ravings; I attributed them instead to one "Gary Pike," local firebrand, all-American crank, and, yes, fictional creation. Since August 1997, I have written regularly for the newspaper as Pike and others—submitting letters, guest "expert" columns, and bogus reporting—concealing myself behind free e-mail accounts. How many fake writers did I invent? About as many as the months I spent working at *The Business Journal* full-time.

In my spare time I manufactured whole companies. They emerged from my head wildly profitable and fully staffed with ambitious assistants obeying the bidding of sage bosses. If my fictional characters filed tax returns, I probably would have been personally responsible for creating more new jobs in central New York than any non-fictional company.

I littered my fictions with references, allusions, and bastardized quotations from literature, less to show off my fine education than to underline how utterly irrelevant it now seemed. I quoted Donald Barthelme but made the words pass through the dead lips of Adam Smith. Having just read *Mason & Dixon*, I inserted the opinions of T.R. Pynchon, knowingly citing him as an American historian and author of the monograph *A Most Intoxicating Liquid: A History of Coffee, the Coffee Bean, and Coffee Houses in Pre-Revolutionary America*. In another counterfeit, I drew names of characters from a *New York Review of Books* essay about Vincent Van Gogh forgers and the businessmen who knowingly peddled the knock-offs.

As Paul Maliszewski, I continued to report on quarterly figures and tepidly gauge the effects of proposed regulations. My fake characters, however, were free to engage business issues with everything from unhinged speculation to dimwitted appeals to common sense. I granted my characters as many titles ("a consultant for middle-middle and upper-middle managers in the Los Angeles metropolitan area") as tangled points of view and rhetorical tics. In this age of memoir and conspicuous confession, I adopted more than a dozen identities, none of them very truthful but all of them, curiously, found worthy of publication. I was Gary Pike, Samuel Collins, T. Michael Bodine, Carl S. Grimm, Grimm's assistant Simone Fletcher, Noah Warren-Mann, Irving T. Fuller, Daniel Martin, and Pavel R.

by paying more attention to the dictates of demographics and focus groups. As they become less elitist and more in touch with the people, they must also adopt the intellectual convictions of the business world: that markets are democracy; that social conflict is dysfunction. What is required is a sort of unilateral cultural disarmament, an intellectual laissez-faire. If abandoning its brief dalliance with "cynicism" is the price of saving journalism from a catastrophic loss of status, then it's a bargain. So in a business that has always been schizophrenic, a place both of angry outsiders and the arrogance of power, of protests and of platitudes, public journalism comes down solidly on the side of the latter: It is Eddie Guest over H.L. Mencken, Roger Rosenblatt over Murray Kempton.

Of course, it is impossible to doubt the good intentions of the public journalists. And surely one must acknowledge that any number of efforts described as "public journalism" have enjoyed signal successes: *The Kansas City Star*'s 1995 series on urban sprawl, for example, is an outstanding example of critical, community-minded reporting. But consider how neatly public journalism's dreams of a new consensus dovetail with the other journalistic "reform" tendency of the Nineties—the corporatization of the news. Although both movements come to their conclusions through different logical routes, both insist on transforming newspapers into demographic reflections of their readership and on excising the odd (and often anti-corporate) voices of idiosyncratic editors and publishers. It is no coincidence that Mark Willes, CEO of Times Mirror and a self-proclaimed public journalist, pulls the plug on the excellent *New York Newsday* (for less than convincing bottom-line reasons) and all but merges advertising and news departments at the *Los Angeles Times*, while passing his deeds off as civic duty. What he's doing is facilitating conversation, you see, using the proven democratic machinery of marketing to let the people of Los Angeles see themselves in all their glorious peopleness. And please understand: Elitists aren't those who run the world; they're those who criticize the CEOs.

Tycoon on a Bus: The Practice

IF the rage for public journalism can be understood as a contest to shout "The People, Yes!" louder than the next guy, then the newspapers produced by the Gannett Corporation must be understood as the least cynical and the most civic-minded of them all. Certainly the company has made remarkable claims along these lines. In 1996 Robert Giles, then editor and publisher of Gannett's *Detroit News,* offered this definition of what public journalism meant to him:

> "It is a way to keep the reader's voice in our minds. We are constantly meeting with our readers, conducting focus groups to discover not only what broad areas they are interested in but what specifically is on their minds, what they want us to engage. What is it they want their newspaper to do?"

What Giles's newspaper was doing, specifically, was teaching its union employees a thing or two about the new market order on the streets of Detroit and Sterling Heights, Michigan.

Unless you happen to be a worker on the receiving end of its flexibility strategies, or a reporter at a newspaper that competes with one of its products, it is unlikely that you've ever thought too much about Gannett, the nation's largest newspaper chain and publisher of *USA Today.* So well-camouflaged a part of the American landscape are its various newspapers that Gannett sometimes seems virtually invisible. And yet Gannett is precisely where those concerned about the future of journalism should be looking. Not only has the new middlebrow imagined by the theorists of public journalism here been refined to perfection, but in Gannett's hands it has also become an ideology of corporate power. An empire of uplift, an autocracy of interactivity, Gannett has fashioned over the years a perfect synthesis of cultural populism and corporate predation.

When figures from across the profession denounce "cynicism," Gannett newspapers are most definitely not what they have in mind. A survey of several recent editions turned up such innocent page-one fare as stories about the travels of the Chicago Bulls chaplain (*Rockford Register-Star*), a battery-powered lollipop holder (*Des Moines Register*), the Beanie Baby bubble (*Cincinnati Enquirer*), the man who introduced the corn dog to Iowa

Liberman, and no one, from the publisher, the editor, and my fellow writers to the advertisers whose ads appeared next to my fictions, ever had a clue.

The Business Journal, November 10, 1997

To the Editor:

I write this in the wake of the Dow's terrible fall.

Today [Oct. 27] the Dow fell. Today the Dow fell 550 points. And yet I do not write in sadness, bitterness, anger, or sorrow. Nor do I write to vent my spite or seek my vengeance for that most horrible wrong ever, and yet so very routinely brought against the living—the loss of money, spending power, and capital. Rather, I write to pledge my faith to the Dow and to the wisdom of the market for which the Dow stands as a symbolic, statistically real representation. I also write to express anew, and loudly even, my faith in the Dow as the embodiment of the wealth and economic vigor of this country. Let everyone know: This crash is a test of each of us, investors all. The Dow is merely testing us. To be sure, we must respond properly, not with hesitation, indecision, and heartless dalliances with the bond market (Woe unto any who dally circumspectly in the bond market!), but with the utmost grace and patience— that rare sort of saintly patience of one who finds real joy in counting money three, four, and five times over again until one is 120-percent positive of the sum total of money in each stack. Today the Dow fell 550 points, and I have only one question: Are we or are we not faithful investors? Before you answer, think, for we cannot be merely lukewarm. The Dow will not tolerate lukewarm investors, nor should it.

Of only one thing can we be certain: The Dow has fallen before and it will fall again. I was recently invited by the Syracuse *Post-Standard* to contribute my thoughts for its coverage of the 10th anniversary of Black Monday, another day that tested our collective faith in the market. While the paper chose to run a report from one of the wire services instead of the local story, readers may be

Continued on page 20

(*Des Moines Register*), and several cautionary entries pointing out that the rides at state fairs can make you dizzy (both *The Louisville Courier-Journal* and *The Des Moines Register*).

In fact, the campaign against cynicism in news— and the tendency to conflate criticism with "elitism"—

Continued on page 75

March Ample Life

Methought I saw my late live-in theory
    crossing the fireplace like a train

For the Headless Horseman is bald
    in the grave where the hair grows long

And Maud was the androgyne without a club
    on the path to Willy Beach

Dear George, the attitude was glued
    myopic and is a myopic clue

Dear Lesbia, dyslexia lives
    The schizophrenics clap for their sunup

But what is the name of your parrot?
    We'll call it Carriage for Two

Squeak, dear parrot, sing
    etcetera, a number of songs etc.

Illusory Town where Mad Tom lives
    whose lungs are fucked by God and such

Where signal fires code Aurora
    referring to just another ducking

Lake at the edge of sleep
    the deathless equestrienne sees

Her namesake singing his hunger
    as one spouse signs for another

Sorting out this endless fragment of sky
    the curtain has hung on our roots

—Stephen Rodefer

THE GAUDY AND DAMNED
Tom Vanderbilt

JUST off Highway 126 in Ventura County, California lies the town of Piru. Tucked among the orange groves and foothills of the Santa Clara valley, it is a strikingly well-preserved small town, the kind of place urban theorists dream about and on which towns like Disney's Celebration community are modeled. Piru's Center Street brims with quaint structures. One rustic clapboard building bears the faded legend "Earl's Feed and Seed," and below that, the spunky notation: "Started 1932 . . . Still Going." A few blocks ahead is the town's central business strip, a Twenties-era row of ten or so buildings, each with quaint signs announcing "bank" or "barber shop."

Piru has only one problem. There never was an "Earl's Feed and Seed." The bank, as well as the barbershop, is empty. Aside from a convenience store and the honky-tonk Piru Cantina a few doors down, the street is absolutely dead. There is a Twilight Zone feel to the place, as if the town's residents suddenly pulled up stakes one day fifty years ago and left things pretty much as they were. Or maybe "Potemkin village" is a better metaphor: Down-

town Piru, it turns out, exists mainly to provide film and television directors with the Mayberry-like small town feel their products require. Whether serving as Athens, Georgia in a film about Tina Turner or as some timeless community in a Disney film, Piru has flourished as a setting for Hollywood productions. And when the film companies pull out, Center Street goes back to being a mostly vacant strip in an economically struggling small town.

Piru's ties to the film industry go back many years. The proprietor of a local museum showed me a Piru hotel register from 1911 that included the names D.W. Griffith and Mary Pickford, who were in town to make the silent film *Ramona*. In later decades everything from *The Defiant Ones* to *Murder, She Wrote* was shot here. But Piru was also, all those years, a town with a functioning business district of its own. By the Nineties, though, Piru's downtown was a shell of its former self. The 1994 Northridge earthquake dealt it the final blow, rendering most structures on the town's main strip uninhabitable. Most businesses—including a real bank—closed, unable to afford the cost of repairs. In 1995, Ventura County secured just under $400,000 in federal disaster relief funds for Piru. The buildings were earthquake retrofitted and otherwise made inhabitable again.

But no businesses came back, and Piru's commercial strip is now basically a federally subsidized film location. "It was not the intent to preserve the buildings strictly as a film set," says Mary Ann Krause of the Ventura County supervisor's office. "It's a kind of result of businesses not moving back in." Krause points out that Ventura County has targeted Piru as a "redevelopment area," although options for a small, low-income town made up largely of migrant agricultural workers are limited. The community sorely needs a bank, Krause notes, but banks claim that given the town's size (its population is below 2,000), even an ATM would cost more to maintain than it would generate in revenue.

So Hollywood is the only show in town: Fully forty productions a year are filmed here. Unfortunately, the attentions of producers and the doings of cameramen do not an economy make. Even though revenue from county film permits ($325 per day) funds a neighborhood council, most of Piru's take from the industry goes to the owners of the buildings that are used. Not surprisingly, there has been antagonism between the locals, who regard film companies as arrogant interlopers disrupting town life, and Hollywood production companies, who regard locals as greedy gougers, eager to squeeze a buck out of them. A local neighborhood film liaison has helped smooth relations between the town and the film companies, and the property owners who once had to worry about their tenants' business being affected have warmed to location shooting. "The owners of the buildings aren't concerned" about the town's lack of businesses, says one longtime Piru resident. "They're getting more money now than they ever were before."

Piru never stars as itself in movies, so unlike the New York of David Letterman or the Madison County of the bridges, it exerts no attraction on tourists. "That's the whole irony of it—the town loses its identity in the film," says Matthew Coolidge, director of the Center for Land Use Interpretation, whose group has been photographing Piru's transformations at the hands of Hollywood. And yet in a peculiar sense the town's metamorphosis from actual town into film set makes good economic sense—a fact the residents themselves acknowledged in 1995 when they brought in a member of the California Film Commission to advise them on how to make the town a more appealing film location. After all, moviemaking is Los Angeles's main industry; soon it will be larger than the state's electronics and aerospace industries combined. Location filming expanded nearly 10 percent in the Los Angeles area last year, and Hollywood's search for office and studio space has pushed vacancy rates in areas like Burbank as low as 5 percent and nearly doubled rents in some areas. In the new simulacral economy, Piru offers two "comparative advantages": It provides a cheap setting in which to "outsource" place, and its look can be easily altered to suit specifications.

"The real now imitates the imitation," writes architecture critic Ada Louise Huxtable in *The Unreal America*. "Towns are remaking themselves, and developments are casting themselves in the theme park image, given a stage-set presence from a look to a complete concept carried out to the last 'authentic' touch." The movies dress up Piru in the guise of some fictional place, while other towns dress themselves up to present a commodified version of their own history that makes the town look like a film set. Oddly enough, what makes Piru (described in one newspaper account as "cut right out of the American dream") so scenic and desirable is its economic stagnation, which has kept the growth (read: sprawl) that marks so much of the county from encroaching on its small-town charm.

Where Piru has a real history, other new developments springing up across the country come prepackaged with their own imagined histories. The new Andres Duany-designed development of Riverside in northwest Atlanta has invented a history for itself going back to the Civil War. "We'd love for that history to be true. But we didn't have the history here, so we're creating our own," a resident told *The Wall Street Journal*. Conveniently located near high-tech job centers and good schools, imagined communities provide instant roots and tradition. It's only a short step from there to the "imagineering" of the film studio theme parks, where sets that only existed as fiction can be visited as real places.

As I pulled out of Piru, the parking lot of "Earl's Feed and Seed" was

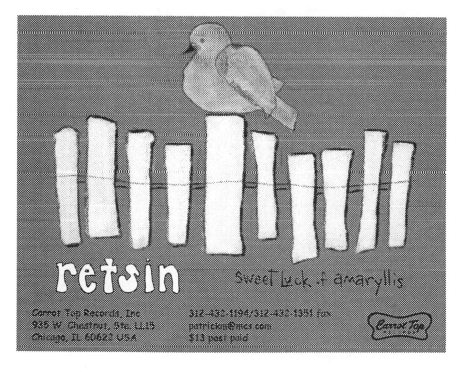

playing host to a three-person crew filming a music video. The singer strummed a guitar under the faded sign, no doubt in search of an authentic, down-home backdrop for the global marketing of his music. But how strange is all this, really? The layout of Los Angeles itself was determined by the spatial needs of studio lots, where outlandish vernacular architecture reigned supreme, and where a film company recently built a shopping promenade that re-created a "real" Los Angeles street. In Piru, this logic is simply coming home to Mayberry.

As small towns struggle to find new sources of wealth in an economy of images and information, it comes as no surprise that their look should prove their most tangible asset.

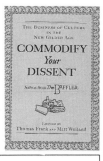

American Heartworm

BEN METCALF

I.

I proceed from rage: rage at those whose ignorance, either God-given or self-consciously homespun, has excited in them a wrongheaded desire to peddle as the font of all that is virtuous and productive and eternal about our nation that shallow and putrid trough we call the Mississippi River. For generations we have suffered such fools to create unworthy riverside wetland areas and disappointing overlook sites and unventilated paddleboat museums and disturbing amusement parks on the theme of the American frontier; to form historical societies so that we might come to think a great deal more than we should of a rill no deeper in places than a backyard swimming pool and far less apt to hold its water; to lay bicycle paths along the levees so that we might crack open our heads within sight of chemical wastes bound for the Gulf of Mexico; to clutter the calendar with steamboat festivals and "Big Muddy" days so that we might pay a premium for corndogs and warm cola, and grow red and sullen under the Midwestern sun, and slap our children before a congre-

gation of strangers acquainted with the impulse and approving of the act. Yet as much as I detest those who would pound the pig iron of history into the tinfoil of folklore, and despite the ease with which I could build a case against these people, and ascribe all that is trumped-up and harmful and loathsome about their region to a native failure to work the algebra of decency and taste, my hatred of the Mississippi itself is greater still, and conscience will not let me sight the lesser target.

For what manmade entity has worked more evil upon the land than has this accident of nature? What other waterway has been the seat of more shame, or has inspired us to greater stupidity, or has inflicted more brutal and embarrassing wounds upon our culture? Have not the basest qualities to be found in the people of the middle states been quickened by the river's example, or by its seeming impulse for self-promotion? And have not these lessons been learned so well that the region now has little more to recommend it than the various log-cabin homes of Abraham Lincoln

Continued from page 12

interested in my comments, particularly in light of today's small corrective crash.

I remember well October 19, 1987. I recall watching in grim, unabashed terror as the Dow plunged to new lows. So low. I had tried periodically during the day to reach my broker. The phone, I realized in an epiphany, perhaps for the first time (though I can't be sure), was the instrument by which I can reach the Dow and communicate my instructions to it. But not that afternoon and not that day. I wanted to sell, but couldn't get through— couldn't, in fact, get any answer. I called and called, but the Dow said nothing in return, answering only in silence and the mocking tone of a busy signal. In retrospect, I am glad I stuck by the market, continued to invest vigorously, and maintained the level of my faith in the Dow.

In wars, nobody ever reports the good news. This truth is no less true of the days when financial markets result in ruin for some people. Few reporters reported the small recoveries during the day. Do you know on Black Monday, the Dow climbed between eleven and a little after noon and again after one and once more just before three o'clock? Few do. Why does nobody speak of these recoveries? Surely in today's crash, the same is true. Were you to sit down and plot the Dow's movements over 15- to 30-minute intervals, the story would be more complicated, far richer even than is contained in the word "crash." Remember that in recoveries there is hope, even in small ones. All recoveries, even less-than-one-point upticks, contain signs spoken directly to the faithful and audible to those awake to hear. (Those who can discern while blindfolded a one-dollar bill from a twenty by the sounds they make certainly know of what I speak.)

The year before Black Monday, my wife and I bought my son stocks for his birthday. We selected for the boy's very first investment Microsoft—a small num-

(hundreds of these), a handful of competing grain-based gasoline concerns, and the fat substitute Olestra? But I hardly mean to confine myself to generalities here: My grievances against the river are specific and they are personal, for so thoroughly have the ideals it teaches laid waste to the soul and imagination of my own family, the Metcalfs of southern Illinois, that a high degree of emotional suffering and moral decay has become almost a point of pride among its members as they walk life's dreary dirt road.

II.

THE Mississippi's lessons are not "hard" in the familiar sense, wherein some touching bit of wisdom is had for a nominal fee, payable in humility and gratitude; they are hard precisely because, being wholly bad lessons, they exact a cost in wisdom, and because the river's students pay a dear tuition in sanity and health and self-esteem for the privilege of learning that which can only harm them further. Moreover, history records an almost conscious effort by the "old man" to clear his classroom of all those who recognize bunk when they see it and to gather in those who do not, a task accomplished in large part through the importation of white men. The first of these, De Soto, saw the river in 1542 but was of a reasonable bent and did not think the discovery worth bragging about; the river killed him. One hundred and thirty-one years later came Marquette the priest (now a Wisconsin basketball power) and Joliet the salesman (now an Illinois prison), who canoed downstream despite being asked not to by the local Indians and who, along with La Salle et al., set in motion a process by which the hospitable natives of the area became first trinket wholesalers, then Christians manqué, and finally a market to saturate with whiskey and firearms. Once this last goal had been achieved, the Choctaw helped the French annihilate or enslave the Natchez, while the Ojibwa scattered the Sioux, drove off the Winnebago, and ran the Fox, already shot full of holes by the French, into the desolate reaches of northeastern Wisconsin, where the Packers now play. Then arrived the European smallpox in 1782, ably ferried from village to village by the obliging Mississippi, and what few natives the plague left breathing were thereafter loath to crane their necks around the bend for fear of what was coming to get them next.

I imagine that after such a convincing bit of treachery only the stubborn or the foolish would not make some effort to get as far away from the river as they possibly could. One of those who stayed, or was born of those who stayed, was my great-great-great-grandmother "Grutch," most likely a Chickasaw, who married Joshua Metcalf, a widowed southern Illinois farmer, and bore him a son, Frank, to complement the lot his dead wife had left him, and who died herself, along with the first wife's children and those of a neighboring farm couple who had asked her to babysit, when at lunchtime one day she poured out tall glasses of milk laced with rat poison. The neighboring parents were never seen again, and it is assumed that they poisoned the milk and the children much in the same way that an animal chews off its own foot to be free of a trap, the trap in this instance being the river and all that it had cost them.

Young Frank did not fancy milk and drank only half of what was in his glass, enough to stunt and disfigure him but not enough to discontinue the line. In spite of his flaws, and his half-breed hair and features, the boy managed to secure a local farm girl for a mate and to avoid her outraged brothers, who had sworn vengeance not for the insult of the seduction but because a general by the name of Metcalf had once enthusiastically slaughtered their Irish cousins at the behest of the English crown. Frank tilled the soil in southern Illinois as had his father before him, leaving only briefly to make some ranching money in the Indian Territory (later Oklahoma) but returning when the Arkansas, a tentacle of the Mississippi, dried up one summer, as did the sum of his herd and profit.

My great-grandfather, Otto, was just a boy when he watched his father's fortune blow away in the Oklahoma dust, and when he grew into manhood all the obstinacy of his forebears, and all the bitterness and disappointment this trait had sowed over the generations, took full root in him. Otto sought to revisit his father's dream without leaving Illinois, *without leaving the river*, and because he could not afford the acreage required to graze even a moderate herd there, and

ber so as not to spoil him. That year everyone in an investing way was excited about Microsoft, and besides, my son showed an early, heart-warming interest in the workings of computers, particularly the creation of clever, memory-resident Windows-based applications for those working in home-office business environments. My son, it also must be said, shares with Microsoft CEO Bill Gates a birthday, October 28. Tomorrow, coincidentally enough. (But in this age of the Dow, may anything rightly be said to be a coincidence?)

We couldn't just buy the boy stocks for his birthday, however. For how long and loudly would he have howled at that rough, unkind outrage? He's a boy, after all. So my wife and I bought him a basketball to go with the stocks.

The evening of the crash I telephoned my son at school, and I said to him, "Son, the Dow has crashed, son. Your basketball's now worth more than your stock." This was, of course, a bit of an exaggeration on my part, though Microsoft stock did drop 19.25 points to 45.25 by the close of trading that day.

The value of a thing is determined only by a buyer and a seller who find a price which both believe agreeable. The faiths of the buyer and seller support this value. Even after today's crash, the value of all shares on the New York Stock Exchange is more than $8 trillion. It is estimated that $2 trillion of this value was added in the last year during the Dow's meteoric rise to the highest heights it has known. Similarly, the value of the economy may be calculated by the price of the goods and services it produces. This year that value is approximately $7 trillion. Since the economy grew less than 4 percent last year, it may be said that the value of goods and services added in the last year is $280 billion. Only realists and fools dare to suggest that, because $280 billion is less than one-seventh of the increase in claims on the Stock Exchange, the Dow and the market that it embodies are grossly inflated in value. Realists and fools are of no concern to investors, those individuals who move adroitly in the dark, guided by faith, those who sustain the market with their belief in the market. Today the Dow fell 550 points. I write to ask each of you to maintain along with me your faiths in the Dow.

Gary Pike, Syracuse, N.Y.

On Tuesdays before an issue of the newspaper went to the printer, Norman Poltenson, *The Business Journal*'s publisher, would give me his latest editorial for proofreading and comment. The rest of the paper was usually complete but for a yawning white space reserved for him on page four. His byline and a short note about upcoming personal appearances (a minute or so weekly on a local TV news broadcast, at 6:45 A.M.) would already be laid out and, along with the other pages, hanging on either side of a long, narrow hallway for staff inspection. Poltenson's picture, a heavily shaded pencil drawing that I thought of as a very distant and very poor cousin of those copper-plate engravings in *The Wall Street Journal*, would look down from the top of the third column, surveying the thirty column inches of nothingness.

Poltenson the man would be upstairs in his office, writing to exact length. He was more familiar with printing than writing and seemed to take a kind of pride in converting the number of unfilled column inches on page four into a frighteningly close

because this circumstance served only to affirm his small place in the world, he made a habit of reversing the inevitable stampedes with shotgun blasts; all that could not be controlled in this manner he struck out at with his fists.

His firstborn, Max, tolerated these outbursts and the whippings because he believed, incongruously, that his place in the world was not small but large. He rode boxcars and flew cropdusters and caroused and married and in the end could no more escape the river's gravity than had his ancestors. Max's large place in the world had convinced him to people it as best he could, and with thirteen mouths to feed, my father's wide among them, he was forced at last to take work along the river as a conductor on the same north-south freight trains that as a young man he had jumped and that a century earlier had killed off the steamboats, which had killed off the keelboats, which had killed off the flatboats, which had killed off the Indians. After nearly two decades of sitting idle in cabooses, catching sight now and then of the Mississippi and all the while smoking tobacco, trade in which the river had graciously abetted, my grandfather was stricken with cancer and found himself being driven, in what the clownish side of circumstance had arranged to be a De Soto, across the muddy water to a hospital in St. Louis, where, after a devastating operation, he would taste the painkillers that in time would weaken first his will, and then his heart, and then his earthly grip.

III.

IN the mid-Seventies an aunt and uncle were part of a Ma Barkeresque gang whose sad tale ended one afternoon with a raid on a warehouse by local authorities and a standoff in which my pregnant, foul-mouthed, shotgun-wielding aunt used up what social credit was still being extended to the family in those days. My own father has said, with some regret in his voice, that he once passed up the opportunity to help rob the Denny's between Charleston and Mattoon, Illinois. He had no moral qualms with the plan but could not find the energy to participate, or to do much else over the next twenty-odd years, once he understood how little a week's take at the only place in the area worth robbing would improve his ability to feed and clothe his children.

What tripped up my aunt and uncle, and I suspect would have undone my father as well, was an irrepressible urge to brag about what had been stolen and to exaggerate its worth well beyond the bounds of good sense. The police might not have troubled themselves with the warehouse, which of course had been left unlocked, had they not been led to believe that they would find there countless stolen Cadillacs, bags full of laundered mob money, and stacks of Fort Knox gold. As it was, and no doubt owing to the truculent stupidity the river had bred into the Metcalfs over the generations, my aunt made her stand over a few broken-down refrigerators and a lone pig.

Most of America's national resources, and the despoliation of same, have their mythic personifications: the Northwestern forests have Paul Bunyan, who, like the trees he felled, was immensely tall and who, if we are to believe the American lumber industry, created all that we now see before us; the Great Plains have Pecos Bill, whose bronco rides were apparently so intense that they whipped up the tornados that now regularly flatten trailer parks filled with Metcalfs; and I suppose all of America lays claim to John Henry, who represented the railroad, which has always wanted us to regard it as a natural resource. To this list the Mississippi adds an unmedicated schizophrenic named Mike Fink, a flatboat pilot who, to hear him tell it, was "half horse, half alligator" and could eat "you for breakfast, your folks for supper, and all of your cousins for a snack in between," which is to say that the river is personified, and aptly so, by a stunted and belligerent liar.

The damage done to my family by this monster Fink, and by Huck and Tom, those young liars Fink prefigured, is close to immeasurable. When my father speaks of a youthful altercation, he does not say that both parties were injured some, as is the usual way with fights; rather he says, "I hit that motherfucker so hard he actually complimented me on it later—said he was shitting teeth for a week." When I hear the tale of how my great-uncle Walter threatened my grandfather with a knife, I am not told that there was some nod toward calm, or some recognition that Walter was mentally ill and needed to be dealt with accordingly; I hear that "Max had that silly fucker on his knees before he could

approximation of the number of words required, all in his head. Poltenson had come to publish the newspaper not as a writer or an editor, but as the inheritor of his family's printing business, which he and his brother decided to sell. Starting the newspaper consumed most of Norman's share of the proceeds; buying a competing newspaper (in order to put it out of business) took care of the rest. By the time I began working at *The Business Journal*, the paper reached about 9,000 readers in sixteen counties across central and upstate New York—business owners mostly, whose names were culled from a Dun & Bradstreet database and who received their subscription gratis. It was the ideal journalistic stepping stone to not much of anything.

When he finished his latest editorial, Poltenson would come looking for me. "Mr. Maliszewski," he would say, "if you would be so kind as to read this over and offer your comments to me with your usual alacrity, I would appreciate it." For the next half hour I would grind my teeth and stomp my feet and pound my desk over howlers like "Any attempt to 'humanize' the corporation should be dismissed as syrupy, corrosive sentiment." Though I'd point out all the holes in his arguments I had the patience to find, Poltenson only seemed to want a thorough proofreading. He would listen patiently as I expressed my disbelief that, say, mutual funds were society's great equalizer, but then thank me and accept only my stylistic suggestions.

Out of this climate were born Gary Pike and Samuel Collins, my two writers of letters to the editor. Both debuted in the same issue, writing in response to a predictable Poltenson editorial on OSHA regulations. All the covert ideological cargo Poltenson slipped by on a raft of ill-gotten statistics, Pike would hail loudly as righteous and true. Collins wrote only on those occasions when I was so angry I couldn't be bothered to invent a satirical perspective.

As the fake letters became more frequent and windy, the white space available to Poltenson dwindled. Finally, one of Pike's letters managed to kick Poltenson off the page altogether. This was not good. Although I enjoyed seeing the editorial page—always home to dozens of statistical fictions— become a venue for my real fiction, it bothered me that my counterfeits allowed Poltenson to skip out on a column or two. Clearly, I had to change tactics. My characters would need to become full-fledged contributors to *The Business Journal*, develop their own subjects and make forays into expert columns and perhaps even the news section, a kind of promised land for the faker.

As my hackwork piled still higher, I began to think of journalism not as a series of unique assignments or stories, but as a limited number of ideas and conventions which each story had somehow to affirm. When Poltenson assigned me to write about tort reform legislation proposed by "New Yorkers for Tort Reform," a faux grassroots effort led by major manufacturers, he suggested I interview a few of the reformers, talk to a trial lawyer, and then write it up with the usual on-the-one-hand-on-the-other-hand equivocation. In the hands of a trained journalist, such back-and-forth disagreements write themselves and can be as long or short as the editorial requirements of the moment. But such a standard telling of the story also includes little or no context or historical perspective, and the reader is left with nothing but a sense of muddled ambivalence. Every story's a toss-up.

But after looking into New Yorkers for Tort Reform, I decided to write about a survey they had commissioned, showing

blink and told him, 'If you ever pull a knife on me again, you sonofabitch, I'll stick it so far up your ass you won't have to cut your meat come suppertime.' "

I do not know exactly what led Walter to draw on Grandpa. By all accounts Walter was a miserable drunk who spent his days whitewashing clapboard houses that eventually would rot because of the flooding and the humidity, and would collapse into sticks if a twister came near, but could not be built of stone or brick because the boy in Mr. Twain's story had painted a *wooden* fence, and so Walter, who might have made a decent and sober bricklayer, was forced instead to cover house after wooden house with the whitest paint he could find, which contained an extraordinary helping of lead, which may or may not have given him the bone cancer that would eventually spread to his skull and torture him there until he died but certainly did not help his sanity or intelligence in the meantime and may have been a factor in both the drinking and the knife pulled on Grandpa. I do not know. What I do know is that Walter might have lived and died beyond humiliation's shadow if the river had not driven him to drink, and Tom Sawyer had not poisoned him with lead, and Mike Fink had not encouraged him to pull a knife on a man three times as fast, ten times as smart, and fully twice his size.

IV.

I used to consider it odd that the word most often called upon by those compelled to describe their feelings for a river that had just washed away their crops, or their homes, or their livestock, or their neighbors, was "respect," because to my mind a river worthy of respect put up a fight against the rain, and made some show of absorbing what fell, and did not run its banks at the first sign of darkening clouds and heat lightning. I did not know then that to the river's victims, "respect" is but a theatrical means of invoking the notions "fear" and "helplessness," and that so familiar are these notions to the river-warped mind as to render a more direct reference to them absurd.

Fear in the Midwest bears relation not only to the river's senseless attacks but to the flattened land beyond its banks, which promises the paranoid (and the river has made many of these) that he will be able to see Armageddon coming a long way off but reminds him always that there will be precious little barring Armageddon's way. My father has said that when lazy old Basil Metcalf, my great-great-great-great-great-grandfather, reached the Mississippi somewhere in the lower half of Illinois, he stopped there simply because it was the first thing he had encountered since leaving the East that could not be walked around or over; he intended to press on, the story goes, but perished before he could decide whether to head north or south. His son Reuben, an uncommonly bleak and wary soul, father of Joshua, in time would see a son taken away by the Union Army and would sit outside his farmhouse and scan the horizon until one morning he spotted what he took to be a visitor far across his fields and by evening held a note informing him that his son was dead, shot through the eye at Vicksburg, the body being sent upriver to Cairo. Reuben set off to claim the boy's remains, sure now that fate and the landscape had conspired against him, and promptly vanished. He may have reached Cairo and kept going, having concluded too late that his father's course need not have been stayed by such a petty obstacle, but more likely he was murdered somewhere along the river's banks, a common occurrence in those days and not unheard of in these. At any rate, the river failed to make delivery on either corpse.

The Midwestern strain of helplessness is in part a function of the river's exaggerated capacity, for although much is made of the fact that it attains a width of 3,000 feet (generally rounded to "a mile") and a depth of 200 feet (also "a mile"), this holds true only if one attempts to swim across in the vicinity of New Orleans; upstream the soundings are less impressive. Above Cairo a shipping channel of just twelve feet is maintained, and above Minneapolis this figure shrinks to a mere nine. It is well worth asking what chance nine or even twelve feet of depth have against a flow of the sort reported in 1993, when eleven times the volume of Niagara Falls threatened St. Louis, and it is equally well worth asking what chance is afforded even inland trailer homes against a river so ill-equipped to contain the water, or to teach by its example anything more hopeful than that weakness and chaos are the natural law.

how the study's results came from outrageously worded questions. I had only recently started to work at the paper and had unfortunately not yet mastered the forms. Poltenson slugged the story as "analysis," which seemed to me like an apology or a warning label. Analysis, I gathered, was not one of the traditional forms at *The Business Journal*. As I learned to stop worrying and love the forms, I also came to appreciate their efficiency. No matter how contrary and damning the information I unearthed in interviews and research, a couple turns of the crank ensured that it all came out looking as indistinguishable as the next story and the next story and the next story.

When I heard about *The New Republic* fabulist Stephen Glass, I thought I had found a co-conspirator. Here, maybe, was someone else who understood the restrictions of journalism and bristled against them. I earnestly wrote him an e-mail care of his last-known fake company. I described my project as a series of necessary counterfeits and expressed the sincere hope that he too had a satirist's motives. At magazines and newspapers, meanwhile, the hand-wringing and soul searching went into high gear. Presses all along the Eastern seaboard turned out one disingenuous apology after another. Forgive us, readers. This won't happen again. Contrite tenders of the journalistic flame suggested that perhaps young writers should be kept from writing articles with unnamed sources, a signature of Glass's style. They're not old enough to use the power tools.

After spending most of a weekend reading Glass's collected works, however, I decided that his writing was not so much satiric as sarcastic. Not a single article tweaked readers' expectations or questioned received opinion. He only made the conventionally wise seem that much wiser. Glass, it appeared, was nothing more than a master of journalism's simple forms, a kind of superfreelancer. Men's magazines, policy magazines—to Glass they were all just outlets. His writing carefully mimicked the style and form of each one, bowing obsequiously to everything its editors valued. The articles hit all the right targets and confirmed all the right stereotypes. Ever think stockbrokers pay too much attention to Alan Greenspan's every utterance? A Glass article confirms what you suspected, inventing an investment company where the traders kneel before a photograph of Chairman Al. Stay up late fretting over the vast right-wing conspiracy to get the president? Glass reports on one so literal it should have been called "The Right-Wing Conspiracy."

Glass's articles were, as commentator after commentator wrote, too good to be true, but that hardly explains why they were published. Editors didn't judge them to be good articles because they were well-written or moving. They ran Glass's writing, I think, because it did everything that good writing in *The New Republic* is expected to do. A Glass article told you that what you assumed was, in fact, true—young Republicans are visigothic—and it slyly congratulated you on the intelligence of your suspicions. The combination of colorful tales buttressing cherished assumptions was so potent that everyone who came into contact with his stories desperately wanted them to be true, and so printed them.

The Business Journal approaches stories with exactly the same logic. News stories, for instance, follow several hardened formulas, each affiliated with a popular fictional genre: the merger and acquisition article (best written using the techniques of a romance novel, with the central metaphor of

The power of this lesson is made clear to me when I learn that a cousin of mine has burned down his high school because a bully told him to do so, or has molested a child for his own reasons, or has run off with his brother's wife (but offered his own in recompense), or has deserted his pregnant girlfriend for a woman old enough to buy him beer, or has somehow managed to electrocute himself, or has tattooed an infant, or has been beaten so badly that her kidney was removed, or has not spoken to her aunt since her aunt married the man who ruined the kidney, or has rolled a car because his father never taught him to slow down on corners (and because the thought never occurred to him privately), or has attempted to run down his wife and her lover in a combine, or has been shotgunned in the chest at close range but is "too ornery to die," or has been arrested for growing marijuana *in the front yard*, or has made no effort to pay the telephone bill and must now communicate solely by CB radio, or has become some sort of humorless Christian, or has been delivered of yet another child so that this jug band of woe might play on.

I can no more doubt that the river has turned and perverted my cousins' lives than that it has done the same to its own course, at will and at random, over the eleven thousand or so years since it was brought into existence by what looks to have been an honest mistake on the part of a glacier. In his book *The Control of Nature*, Mr. McPhee writes that "southern Louisiana exists in its present form because the Mississippi River has jumped here and there within an arc of about two hundred miles wide, like a pianist playing with one hand. . . . Always it is the river's purpose to get to the Gulf by the shortest and steepest gradient." Although I concur with the notion that the river's selfish meanderings have cursed us with southern Louisiana, I prefer the image of a drunken blind man carelessly whipping his cane back and forth in unfamiliar surrounds to that of a tasteful pianist. And I do not think that the river's purpose is "to get to the Gulf" so much as it is to cause the greatest amount of suffering on the way there. Consider the river's capricious disregard for the boundaries between our states: Arkansas has been forced to sue Tennessee on numerous occasions (1918, 1940, 1970) in order to retrieve land and taxpayers carved from its eastern flank by the river and handed over to the Volunteer State. Louisiana has sued Mississippi (1906, 1931, 1966) for like cause, and Mississippi has sued Louisiana, and Arkansas has sued Mississippi, and Missouri has sued Kentucky, and Iowa has sued Illinois, and Minnesota has sued Wisconsin, until the very identities of these states have been eroded, and the wisdom of entrusting their shapes to a slithering and deceitful border impeached.

This epidemic of strife and distrust has spread elsewhere, to other rivers and other states (e.g., *Texas v. Louisiana, Missouri v. Nebraska, Nebraska v. Iowa, Indiana v. Kentucky, Virginia v. Tennessee, Maryland v. West Virginia, Rhode Island v. Massachusetts*), and has so intensified our citizenry's penchant for litigation that judges in many fluvial districts no longer have even the time required to perform a marriage or to entertain a bribe. In those areas directly scarred by the Mississippi, neighbors sue one another with a frequency and a fervor that belie the small gains to be had, having learned at the foot of the river hard lessons in desperation that have left them suckers for the bittersweet lies of the American justice system. I consider it a mere accident that to date, and to the best of my knowledge, no Metcalf has sued another Metcalf, and I do not doubt that this fact will reverse itself soon. Already the Midwestern milieu is such that involvement in a petty lawsuit is held to be the height of glamour and achievement and therefore suitable excuse not to hold down a job.

My grandmother once spoke proudly to me of a cousin who had finally "growed up a little." The cause of the improvement was not parenthood, for he was a father many times over, and by numerous women; nor was it some semblance of a career, for he was minimally employed at that time and, as far as I know, since. What impressed my grandmother was that he had found the gumption to sue someone (or to do something that got him sued; I cannot remember which, nor does it particularly matter) and at last stood to make a man of himself. He failed, of course, even on these terms. Petition lost, courtroom fees owed and unpayable, he ceded control to the panic that was his birthright and fled to Missouri, across the river but no farther from it, where

a wedding); the company under investigation (refer to John Grisham's legal thrillers, casting the company as an innocent yet scrappy underdog); the CEO with an unlikely or non-traditional background (fairy tale); quarterly report disclosing surprisingly strong/weak earnings (the vignette, tuned to frequencies of sweetness or sadness, as appropriate); bankruptcy (a real tragedy, mournfully rehearsing the standard business verity that a marketing budget is not to be trifled with); profile of an eccentric (screwball comedy, starring a renegade businessman who walked away from his six-figure salary as a vice president of marketing only to turn to manufacturing decorative mailboxes and—would you believe?—marketing them through mail-order catalogs).

A fictional expert like Carl S. Grimm, who began writing columns for *The Business Journal* in January 1998, seems like any other dispenser of corporate advice. He follows the rules of the genre. He is casually confident, yet serious. He professes bold, counter-intuitive ideas, but remains well-versed in the deployment of clichés. His background mixes equal parts intrigue and prestige: "A former official with both the State Department and CIA, Grimm frequently speaks at overseas engagements for the U.S. Agency for International Development, Andersen Consulting, and the American Federation of Independent Businesses." He's independent. He's successful. He has a book contract with HarperCollins.

What an amazing life Grimm seems to lead. To crisscross borders and time zones in

solitary pursuit of accumulating the most
money possible is certainly close to the
unacknowledged dreams of many readers of
The Business Journal. Were they not
regrettably bound to this earth and these flabby
bodies, to mortgaged homes and long-term
leases on Sevilles, they could surely follow in
Grimm's footsteps. Failing that, readers can
cozy up to his columns, turning to the warm
words of an accomplished expert for the moral
instruction and diversion traditionally found in
genre fiction.

**Carl S. Grimm, "Toward a Life of Pure, 100%
Liquidity," *The Business Journal*, July 6, 1998.**

   *Carl S. Grimm is the author of Liv-
ing Liquidly: How Being More Like
Money Pays Off, which will be published by HarperCollins in fall 1999.
Grimm is a consultant specializing in
currency and trade opportunity analysis, foreign risk assessment, industry
informational surveys, and market-
share projection specification programs. He can be contacted at
csg1137@altavista.net.*

   I suppose the day was like any other,
really. I found myself on the helicopter
from LaGuardia to Kennedy, endeavoring
to bypass the traffic by flying over the city
instead of fighting my way through it.
With total lapsed time well shy of 10 minutes, the cloudless skies of postcards, and
no symptoms of incipient motion-sick-
ness, I was, I must admit, making quite a
success of it.

I suppose he became, at least until the next chance
to play the river's fool* presented, a child again.

V.

THERE runs through this continent a river worthy
at least of the praise heaped upon the paltry
Mississippi; that drains 9,715 square miles of
Canada without once crossing the border as well as
523,000 square miles, or fully one-sixth, of these
United States; that rises up out of the Continental
Divide in Montana and wends its way across the
American heartland, flowing in places north and
elsewhere east and in the balance south, having decided its course a long time ago and having for the
most part stuck to it; that at 2,714 miles is without
challenge the longest stream around and if allowed
by mapmakers to claim its southernmost leg (that
is, "the Mississippi River" below St. Louis) would
reach 3,741 miles, a length bested only by those great
rivers of the Southern Hemisphere, the Nile and the
Amazon. I refer, of course, to the Missouri River.

   In addition to doing its own job, the Missouri drains
nearly three-quarters of the upper Mississippi basin,
leaving the rest not to the Mississippi, which is inca-
pable of doing what by rights should come naturally
to it, but to the Ohio, the Iowa, the Illinois, the Des
Moines, the Wisconsin, the Minnesota, the Meramec,
the Kaskaskia, and the St. Croix, fine rivers all. That
they, along with the White, the St. Francis, the Salt,
and the Rock, should be deemed "tributaries" of the
Mississippi I can only regard as fraud of the highest
order, considering that the Mississippi, which receives
nearly half of its annual flow from the Missouri alone,
and a good deal of the remainder from the Ohio, is but

---

* Mr. Russell "Rusty" Weston Jr., late of Valmeyer, Illinois, and a small pied-à-gulch in Montana, who this past July allegedly took
it upon himself to gun down a dozen cats and two Capitol Police officers before being shot himself, was so perfect an example of
Mississippi victimhood that I wondered at the time of his spree if he did not have some Metcalf blood in him. Here was a man who
had seen his town washed away in the 1993 floods and (stubbornly, pointlessly) rebuilt just a stone's throw to the east to await the
river's next assault, who was terrified of television sets and satellite dishes (this is common even among Midwesterners who own
and enjoy them), who believed that the president of the United States had sent a Navy SEAL to kill him (the SEAL is an unusual
variation here, but the claim of persecution at the hands of the president certainly is not), and whose acute schizophrenia deviated
so slightly from the Midwestern norm that his father thought it sufficient to offer the following gloss to the *Miami Herald*: "His
mind doesn't work real good." More familiar still, and what finally locates Mr. Weston Jr. on the middle bands of the riverine
behavioral spectrum, is his comfort with, and obvious flair for, the lawsuit. In addition to considering a suit against the Secret
Service, who had questioned him regarding threats he had made against the president, Mr. Weston Jr. is known to have sued a
pickup-truck dealer in Illinois and to have fought his eighty-six-year-old landlady, who he claimed had beaten him with a cane, all
the way to the Montana Supreme Court, where, in true Mississippian fashion, he lost.

where these streams happen to collide and not, as is commonly supposed, the mythic force that draws them together or, more ludicrous still, created them.

The Mississippi is in reality a thin creek issuing from a nondescript pond in Minnesota and would likely trickle away to nothing before it reached St. Louis if on the way it did not loot every proper river in sight. Even availed of the extra water, the Mississippi is so wasteful with the stuff, and so fickle with its bearings, that only the constant attentions of the Army Corps of Engineers enable it to reach the Gulf at all. Unaided, it would pour off into the Louisiana swampland known as Atchafalaya and form a fetid inland sea. Should it therefore surprise us that the Mississippi's pupils have developed a habit for public assistance unrivaled even by that to be found in our decaying coastal cities; that there is scarcely a household in my extended family that does not have at least one potential breadwinner sitting it out on some sort of "disablilty"; that there are stores in these people's communities where a food stamp is met with less suspicion than a five or ten dollar bill?

Some years ago an uncle made a break with family tradition and found work in the oil fields near his house, doing so not because he saw any need to improve himself or his situation but because the job allowed him to tell people he was an "oilman," which he thought had a ring to it. He did not care much for the actual work, though, and began to send his eldest son out in his stead, a practice tolerated by my uncle's employers only because they considered it unlikely that the son could be any lazier than the father. The boy soon opened their minds, and one afternoon he arrived home to tell his father, "We've been fired." My parents visited shortly after the incident and found the entire household in good spirits. My uncle had been angry at first, and he did express concern that his son might never learn how to hold down a job, but now he believed that things might work out after all: As he saw it, both he and the boy were now eligible for unemployment. My parents did not disabuse him of the notion.

VI.

HAVING taught the Midwesterner to freeload, and to lie, and to steal, and to work violence against his brother, the Mississippi now rings its doleful school

Along for the ride—in addition to the pilot whose name I forget—was my new friend, whom I'll call Marvin. Poor "Marvin." As Manhattan heaved into sight off to our left, I was commiserating with Marvin, who confided in me how he found himself completely unable to live on $450,000 per year. He had, he claimed, done everything right: educated at a private prep school in Connecticut where the halls are decorated with portraits of past students who became presidents and the classes are attended by young presidents to-be; graduated Harvard with honors and Harvard Law at the very top of his class; been offered a position in more Wall Street firms than he had fingers to count; and been made partner and then senior partner sooner even than his ambitious life-schedule had stipulated. Yet here he was, he said, flat broke and bumming a ride on my helicopter. Strangely, I knew exactly what he meant.

It was later that same day, as the more memorable pieces of my conversation with Marvin bounced and rolled around inside my head like so many shiny coins tossed by well-wishers into a public fountain, that I vowed to achieve a life of pure 100-percent liquidity in order to avoid the fate of "Marvin" and that wretched existence of his. To do so, I had only to make over myself in the image and essential character of money.

On my flight to Jakarta, a few people sat haloed by the harsh dome lights, studying FEER, the *Far Eastern Economic*

Review, and the recently collected reports of the International Monetary Fund. While most everyone else in first-class curled up with *The Financial Times* or rested behind sleep masks, I found the think time to revise my long-term goals, rearranging and reprioritizing. I added one more: Be as liberated as capital itself.

What is the liquid life?

We all know what we mean when we talk of money or capital as liquid wealth; its properties allow it to be applied anywhere for any purpose by anyone who has it. It was Adam Smith, the economist and proto-warrior for free trade, who so presciently wrote, "The practiced accumulation of capital is the topmost taper on the golden candelabrum of existence." Capital, Smith knew, is easily transferable and more widely accepted than a Visa card. The liquid life has in

Continued on page 36

bell once more. My father heeds the call as he always has, emptying the family bank account and driving to one of several riverboat casinos tethered off the coasts of Illinois, Iowa, and Missouri, where he plays at blackjack and roulette until he has entirely lost what sum my mother has managed to save up since his last unfortunate visit. He goes not because he believes that the river will make a winner of him, for he surrendered that fantasy long ago, if indeed he ever entertained it at all. He goes because he believes, or needs to believe, that one day the river might look more kindly upon its son than it has in the past, and teach him some lesson not predicated on havoc and despair, and allow him just once to recoup the losses that have imperiled both his marriage and his sanity.

And of course it never will.

Ecce Mississippi. We might well ask how much longer the republic can stand with a worm such as this slithering through its heart.

Stormy Love Story

MIKE ALBO

I still think about him. You know, my ex-boyfriend, four-star General Norman Paul Schwarzkopf.

It's hard. I was a civilian, he was a general, leading our troops to victory in the Gulf War. To you, to the public, he was sober, fearless, dedicated, loyal. He delivered those great lines like, "We are going to kick their butts," and "Anytime, Hussein Baby."

To me, Norm was love. Huh, he was like the embodiment of love. I have never been as close to someone in my life as I was with him, I swear to God. A lot of people name the name and play the game, mind games, oh I'll call you phone tag, The Dating Game, The Newlywed Game, the Pajama Game, Match Game . . . but few people really know what love is, you know? Because Norman was more than a lover, we were like best friends.

We sort of broke up, you know? We just realized that there were a lot of issues that we both had a lot of problems with and had to deal with.

But for a while there, it was pret-ty go-od!

Picture the scene: 1991, we are deep in the Gulf War.

But it's also the Super Bowl, and the audience, formerly divided and obsessed with their own greedy small selfish concerns, erupts in applause, banded together in patriotism, while Whitney Houston belts out the national anthem. She just sings in her queasily sweet way, in her white hairband and strange wrinkled silk windbreaker warmup outfit and Lady Etonic sneakers. She's always wearing warmups. Why does she always wear warmups? You'd think if you were Whitney Houston you'd wear something tighter or something.

Oh and we're killing people in the Middle East.

But now it's Super Bowl halftime and they roll out a big gooshy centerpiece float of the American Flag and cute little Seth Williams climbs onto it, in his cute little football outfit, holding a cute little helmet, his blond hair shellacked into its own helmet shape on his head, and he sings *his* pigeon-breasted heart out: "Did anyone tell you you're my hero . . . you are the wind beneath my wings," and he's joined by generous, hardworking King of Pop Michael Jackson, who brings with him hundreds of children dressed in various costumes representing the children of the world. And they join little Seth in the song's final verses, and the audience once again erupts in applause!

The Gulf War: a Time of Heroism, a Time of Pain, and a Time of Love.

I met Norman through a mutual friend of ours, Defense Secretary James Baker, just by chance. They came in to this art gallery I was working in to look at some paintings, and immediately we felt the fire of lust—that simple.

Okay, I know you're wondering. It's cut, of course. It's not huge, but it's got a lot of girth and has a perfect banana upturn. But it doesn't taper off.

God his body is so sexy. Harvey Keitel, Robert Mitchum, Joe Piscopo, John Updike, Jack Palance, Michael Landon, Ron Reagan, Danny Glover, Karl Lagerfeld, Ricardo Montalban, Johnny Weissmuller—thick men, smug men, bigoted fucks with crickety barrel frames, muscles packed on their big beef bouillon bulletproof vest bodies.

Nine and a half months we spent together, the nine and a half months of the Gulf War, so long and wartorn, all of America coming together, riveting

Mac-Mahon.

and rationing and looking for the union label to save this great country. And I spent those nine and a half months as Norman's lover, right at his heroic side.

On our first date he took me to his apartment. I sat there very demurely and he opened his closet. He had an entire closet full of those exact tan soupy moonscape desert camouflage leisure suits lined up one after another.

On our second date, he took me to his houseboat and put on this wonderfully sad, sultry music. He told me abruptly to take off my shirt, and then he blindfolded me. I was frightened yet aroused. Clink clink clink, what's that sound? He was clinking the ice in an old highball glass of whiskey he was drinking. He made me lay down on a table and took an ice cube from the glass and traced it down my body. Oooooh! It was so cold!

On our third date, he took me to Coney Island. We went laughing and skipping down the boardwalk. I had a hat on. He tricked me and put me on the Ferris wheel by myself, and made the operator leave me stuck at the top for an hour. Oh Norman how dare you! I am so angry at you Norman Paul Schwarzkopf!

Tee hee hee! Norman buys me balloons, and we go running across the boardwalk. He wears his long black overcoat.

Ha ha ha! Norman dresses me up in a baggy suit and moustache and we go to an ethnic Italian restaurant, and he grabs my penee under the table!

Ho ho ho! Norman and I go to a market of fruits and vegetables, and he seductively picks out various fruits and holds them!

Hu hu hu! Norman fucks me in a dark alleyway, the rain pouring over us, his big saggy square ass jiggling with every thrust!

I'm at work in the art gallery and I am looking at various slides of various art works we're thinking of selling in the art gallery, and I can't get Norman out of my mind so I start masturbating and they begin to flip very very fast and it gets really out of hand!

One time he blindfolds me and takes me into the kitchen and just feeds me different foods...

Mᵃˡ Foch.

Cherry pie filling...a Vlasic pickle...key lime pie...Oh, a jalapeño pepper! *Norman*! It's so *spicy*!

Norman and I had great sex together. He gave me something that I called "The Sensation."

Then, suddenly, in the middle of all this, we like won the Gulf War! Norman called me up. I was so excited, oh Norman we won the Gulf War! All right! We did it we won! U-S-A! U-S-A! U-S-A! U-S-A!

He told me he needed to see me, so I quickly put on my Brooks Brothers shirt and khaki pants and blue sportscoat and blue and orange tie and English Leather. Air Force One sent a helicopter to pick me up and we zoomed over the landscape. "Norman is so psyched to see you!" Jack the Air Force One pilot said. We land in his front yard, and I walk up to the door, he answers it, swinging it open with his big hairy forearms and juicy lovehandles like I remember it.

But something was different. We went for a walk and ended up at a nearby gazebo.

Norman, you're far away—where are you?

The war is over, he said to me, and it's time we went our separate ways.

So. Norman and I broke up. Sometimes I see him ... at the Roxy or the Big Cup, but he's totally different. He's become such a Chelsea Queen. He shaved his chest and wears white tank tops and rolls around on Rollerblades with all his titty tan Chelsea Queen friends.

It's just, it's not like. . . . You know, sometimes I just want to call him up and like tell him he's a big asshole for doing that to me. I just want to say like, Norman, you don't treat people that way . . . there's like a code that humans exhibit to other humans and that's what makes us human and you have no idea what the fuck it's even like to be human, Norman. You are *so* self-obsessed I don't even think you know there are other people around besides yourself. All you do is talk about yourself. I don't think you ever asked me one thing about myself the entire time we were going out. And if you did, it would totally come back to you. Fucker. Can you even discern that there are other objects in the world besides yourself? I don't think so. You know, I really hope you get your act together, Norman—because the way you are now is just scary.

Blood and Pancakes

Service Clubs at Century's End

Dan Kelly

W E are speaking of the over-the-counter Illuminati, my friends; the purveyors of smokers and spaghetti dinners and all things in between. Recite their names three times quickly—Rotary! Kiwanis! Lions Club!—and you risk invoking a suburban bugaboo. Eek! Look there! Do you see them too? Thirty burly, beet-faced men in garrison caps: some shilling teeny bags of peanuts, others flipping flapjacks onto Styrofoam plates—and all bellowing the terrifying shibboleth of "Service, Service, Service!" But don't be afraid, kids, the service club bogeymen can't hurt you anymore. They're sealed away forever with pink aluminum Christmas trees, plastic-wrapped furniture, and all the other failed experiments of Boobus Americanus.

Aren't they?

Service clubs, it goes without saying, are a uniquely American invention. Preceded by nineteenth-century fraternal organizations—the Masons, Odd Fellows, Elks, and others—service clubs offered an alternative to a burgeoning middle class, whose members were unimpressed with the older clubs' promises of freakish rituals, shaky in-

surance policies, and, in the case of the Masons, world domination.

The first true service club was founded in 1905, when Chicago lawyer Paul Harris created Rotary Club. Initially conceived for the bland purpose of improving Harris's networking skills, it was eventually decided that Rotary's true business was Service (always with a capital 'S'). The idea blossomed, and clubs soon sprang up higgledy-piggledy across the nation, and then across the world. With success came copycats: Kiwanis in 1915, and then Lions Club two years later. Whatever their names, "Service!" was their battle cry—a word flexible enough to mean performing any form of charity, from the admirable (serving the blind, as differently abled pinko Helen Keller challenged the Lions to do) to the insipid (taking "widders and orphans" out for a nice lunch). By and large, in their heyday in the Twenties, the clubs threw gobs of money at calamities, "boosted" their hometowns, scratched each others backs, and ate much lunch. Sanctimonious and obscenely gauche, yes indeed; at least they weren't joining another popular club of the day, the Klan. Well, most of them weren't.

Continued from page 30

common with money this freedom of movement. The purely liquid among us are always already willing to move—and move quickly. Liquid-lifers find work instead of allowing work to find them. It's a way of traveling light, acting fast, and staying one step ahead.

People of pure liquid move to where it suits them best, they relentlessly seek their level.

Readers may recall my last letter ["Stock Tip: Invest in Welfare," *The Business Journal*, Jan. 19, 1998], which projected handsome profits in the welfare-management industry, what I called the welfare of welfare. When I wrote that letter five months ago, I was living in Philadelphia. Now I'm in Chicago and in between I've probably lived in three or four more places besides. Perhaps "lived" is not the proper word for what I do, because I stay in luxury hotels, the sort of places where the televisions are not chained to the floor, places at which my arrival is eagerly anticipated, my needs met. Really, I light from assignment to assignment, providing billable advice as I go. I move from hotel to hotel, from Hilton to Holiday Dome to Radisson to Adam's Mark to Hilton again.

The liquid life is a state of mind, really. Sure there are modest costs—e.g., take the wife, who didn't feel she wanted to accompany me on my quest to obtain the liquid life, though she did try it for a while (one month, not to her liking).

An example should bring the liquid state of mind into sharper focus. Follow the money in this quote from *The Financial Times*: "The return of the capital that fled after Beijing's missile tests in the Taiwan Straits in March last year, a relatively accommodating liquidity policy by the central bank and active buying by government controlled funds have brought doubled share values in little more than a year." First of all, congratu-

Nevertheless, the intelligentsia commenced a punching-dummy battle forthwith. H.L. Mencken took special delight in savaging the clubs as cretinous exemplars of the booboisie, who spent their time "worrying about such things as the crime wave, necking in the high schools, the prevalence of adenoids, the doings of the League of Nations, and the conspiracy of the Bolsheviki to seize the United States and put every Cadillac owner to the sword." Another swipe came in the pudgy form of Sinclair Lewis's George F. Babbitt, whose moronic example forever placed the practice of "Babbittry" only a grain or two above necrophilia. Nevertheless, the clubs persisted, hitting their height in the mid-Twenties, then slowly ebbing and flowing into the Seventies. Then, as everyone knows, all their members gathered together and stumbled to the legendary Service Club Graveyard, where they laid down and gracefully expired.

Nah.

Your humble narrator recently made a pilgrimage to his hometown of Oak Forest—a bedroom community five miles southwest of Chicago (eight miles northwest of Park Forest, all you *Organization Man* fans)—to see how the service clubs there were faring. For our suburban expatriate, attending club meetings was somewhat akin to visiting a museum exhibit on the Amish and watching a docent weave blankets on a loom. A living exhibit that appeared stultifyingly dull at first blush, but which slowly unfolded to reveal an immutable devotion to conformity bordering on—dare it be said?—the esoteric. In light of the strain of nostalgia chic currently savaging our culture (see such abominations as the pseudo-swing movement and the Rat Pack's inexplicable canonization), the clubs' stratospheric normalcy approaches a brand of suburban exotica hitherto unimaginable by the hardest-core of hipsters.

Or maybe I'm just not getting enough sleep.

"Service . . . Above Self"

ROTARIANISM: It sounds like a religion, doesn't it? Oh, it is, it is; one populated not by Presbyterians or Catholics, but devout capitalists. Somewhat bereft of the corn pone afflicting other clubs, Rotary's facility has allowed it to slide into the Nineties with more than 1.2 million members, 28,000 clubs, and only a few critical scratches. During the Twenties, cultural highbrows considered Rotary the *ne plus ultra* of organized boobery, and a practical priesthood of American crassness. Aw, heck—the Rotarians I met seemed like Royal Good Fellows; Real Good Mixers, in fact.

Swinging an invitation to a Rotary luncheon was no great trick. My father is a Rotarian, and has been for eleven years. From my perspective, it was a natural progression in an admirable thirty years of hardcore, Grade-A community service, including his stints as a city trustee, alderman, mayor, and now Rotary assistant governor. My father wears duty like a shiny badge, always stopping somewhere far short of True Believer. I keep that in mind for the length of the meeting. Color me slightly biased.

The Rotarians gather in the "private" club room of the House of Hughes, a Swiss chalet-style restaurant in lovely Crestwood, Illinois. The House of Hughes is, in suburban vernacular, a "nice" restaurant (i.e., if you are ten years old, Buster Browns are de rigueur). Foody smells waft about—a mixture of seasoned fries, cube steak, and chicken Kiev—stirring up a mental broth of wedding reception memories. Rotary banners line one wall, each covered in turn with smaller banners from clubs across the globe. At center is a large blue and gold pennant bearing Rotary's symbol (a cogwheel), slogan ("Service . . . Above Self"), and their quadripartite maxim, the "Four-Way Test." Thus:

Of the things we think, say or do:
1. Is it the Truth?
2. Is it Fair to all concerned?
3. Will it build goodwill and better friendships?
4. Will it be beneficial to all concerned?

On a nearby table, a porcupine arrangement of international flags juts from a small display stand. Next to this, a call-to-order bell and a briefcase filled with "Hello, My Name Is . . ." buttons (presumably worn by each member, lest anyone has forgotten who they are since last week). The scene is unspectacular, yet a little strange. One gets the idea that Rotary's trappings have changed little over the past eighty years. They seem less trapped in a time warp than happily nestled in one.

lations are in order—way to go, Taiwan. But let's follow the money, shall we?

The money was afraid of political fall-out from Chinese missile tests. Fair enough, money fled. Money went elsewhere. Money canceled lucrative but tentative deals. Money hopped jets with departing business people or rode electronic wires and flew, trailing more zeroes than you or maybe I can imagine through the money-sphere. But then, you can see what happened next. There's a happy ending here. Money returned. Money marched back into Taiwan like conquering soldiers. Money came home to Mom.

"So what's this all mean?" you ask. When I speak of the liquid life, I speak of a life that abides by the rules of money. If you can do better, be better, and achieve more elsewhere, why then, by gosh, be there, go there, now.

Karl Marx had it only partially right. Labor and capital do obey two unique sets of rules. But Marx could not have foreseen the likes of me and the few people like me. He could not have imagined the way we make airports our living rooms, and their long, glassed-in concourses our entryways. That's us on the phone, conducting business on our laps. That's us playing solitaire on color laptop computers, or taking a chance on the video poker machines that lean down over bars. We go where the money goes, to the new lands of opportunity and investment, looking for financial milk and honey.

Here again is Smith, north star to any thinking economist, "Opportunity is the hearty, weathered sailor on the tumultuous seas of loss and gain." We liquid types go how money goes, by air, at cruising altitudes of 12,000 feet or more, and in first class. Be fearless, be quick, be liquid. Who are we? We are the willfully and meaningfully and lucratively transient, living by silence, exile, cunning—and so on. We always shop duty-free.

What's the opposite of the liquid life?

Four words: routine, attachment, sedentary, and home-body, or R.A.S.H. The opposite of the liquid life is a solid one, and solidity is produced by the above four behaviors and worst of all, solidity causes a rash. A real specter is haunting America at the end of the millennium—the specter of solidity. Remember: solidity is the nightmare from which we are trying to awake. But what happened to Marvin? you ask. Marvin did not live the right life. Poor Marvin. He was too heavy and entirely too solid. Regrettably, his occupation—law—drew him back to earth. The law is fundamentally concerned with representing the legal considerations of bodies, people or corporations. The law is by definition a material pursuit, uses material means to achieve material remedies. Far better to be like money, I say, and trade in information.

Poor Marvin, he couldn't move like money moves. He didn't even seem to recognize himself in my description of the law. When last I saw him, in Kennedy, he merely looked fed-up and annoyed, no doubt angry with himself. Clearly, he appreciated the wisdom in everything I had so unselfishly shared with him about the liquid life, while both on the helicopter and the ground, during the hour or so after that I walked around after him wherever he went.

As for the members, they are exactly as you remember them from all those childhood parades, picnics, and pancake breakfasts. Babbitt's beaming grandsons, *gemütlichkeit* oozing from their pores, march one by one into the room. Wattles, dewlaps, and bellies—all the protuberances of prosperity—spill forth. Surprisingly, only two members wear suits; the new Rotary uniform apparently consists of a sensible ensemble of golf shirt and comfy slacks. Ties are also few and far between, though one stands out, its pattern a jingoist crazy-quilt of American flags. Backslapping, so reviled by Mencken, is still a Rotarian reflex. Of note is the presence of female Rotarians, who slack not in slapping backs, despite being excluded from the XY-chromosome-dominated club until 1989. My hand is repeatedly and vigorously pumped. One Rotarian asks me, "Didn't you work for me once?" Yes, I did. It would be stranger if I hadn't worked high school jobs for half the people here.

My lunchtime table mates, with one exception, are Oak Forest businessmen. On my right is my uncle Jim, an accountant; on my left, Tom the chiropractor. Directly across from me are Paul the optometrist; John, a bus company manager; and Hugh, a retired car dealer. Hugh is a charter member, the club's oldest, and also the man who tells me, without the slightest taint of irony, that when he sold cars, he felt like he was "selling a piece of the American Dream." The aforementioned exception is a former Rotary exchange student from Finland named Maya. Four years have passed since Maya was last a club guest. I know this because the hellishly blonde and achingly lithe Maya is approached by one wolf-eyed Rotarian after another, each gibbering, "This is Maya? Four years . . . I can't believe it's been four years. Well, well, well. . . ."

At 12:10, all babbling is dispersed by the tolling of the bell. In short order, the entire room stands—twenty Rotarians and three guests—and I am reciting the Pledge of Allegiance for the first time since Boy Scouts. Next, we all gravely bow our heads for the recitation of the Four-Way Test and then an aggressively nonsectarian prayer. Finally, my father introduces my mother and me as club guests. I rise slightly, give my best Queen Elizabeth wave to a chorus of hearty hellos, then sit down again. I regret to report that the much-ridiculed practice of "stunts" has not survived. No one, save the women present, is dressed in women's clothing. No spitballs are hurled. No balloons are busted beneath Taftian buttocks.

President Rich opens by announcing that on Memorial Day the club will lay a wreath at the Veterans Memorial at the railway station. This is acceptable to the Rotarians, who murmur warm approval. Next on the agenda, Rotarian Andy distributes the new *Oak Wheel*, the club's newsletter. Many compliments and "Attaboy's" are thrown in Andy's direction, who shows great humility in admitting that he was lucky to have people under him who could make a newsletter. "People who like to use many, many different fonts," I think to myself as I scan the sheet. The newsletter includes a "tidbits" section, sparkling with this bit of pep:

> Rotary District Conference was a success! The club with the highest number in attendance and the highest percent of attendees? OAK FOREST!

Zip! Zowie!

As we dine, I ask my dining companions why they joined Rotary. Paul the optometrist answers in a fog-cutting voice. He signed up back in 1977, after a teacher told him that membership was a terrific way to build business contacts. Eventually, Paul decided that contacts weren't enough; he was more interested in "giving something back to the community." So, following his father's recommendation, he joined Rotary; though in hindsight, joining the Lions would have made more sense.

"Why?" John the bus manager asks blankly.

"Well, because of the eye thing," Paul the optometrist explains.

"Ah," rejoins John, returning to his lunch.

Paul continues, telling me that he's hosted several students in the Rotary youth exchange program.

Um, how exactly does that serve the community, I inquire.

"It helps show the [local] kids that all people are the same all over, really," Paul replies.

Okay, here's another question: What is "Service," exactly? I suddenly grow two extra heads, judging by the looks directed at me.

"Well, the motto is 'Service . . . Above Self,' " Paul chides.

Marvin was not and would never be liquid, but he at least was aware of the liquid life. He said to me, "Carl S. Grimm, I wish I never asked you for a ride."

I've often wondered what it would be like to encounter *Gulliver's Travels* without having any prior knowledge about the book or its author. What if it could be published as a guidebook and shelved in the travel section among all the *Fodor's* and *Lonely Planets*? Tear off the prefaces by the editors, take away the inevitable essay by Allan Bloom, peel back the thin slices of footnotes, and you'd be left with a book that not only fits the form of the travel guide, but that fiendishly parodies it as well. The book's first two editions tellingly carried Gulliver as its author. Swift was absent from the title page.

Believing that satire requires a certain amount of intentional mislabeling, I set out to translate the text of a torture manual used at the School of the Americas into the language and rhetoric of a manager's how-to. With very few changes—substituting "employee" for "subject," for instance—the piece began to look more and more like an advice column. Now published and with nothing whatsoever to announce it as satire, it lies in wait, looking and reading like just another article. In *The Business Journal* it is oddly at home.

T. Michael Bodine, "Don't Get Caught Being a Weak Manager," *The Business Journal*, November 10, 1997.

By T. Michael Bodine

Bodine is a partner, senior business-to-business consultant and Vice President of Marketing, West Coast Operations with Universal Business Consultants (UBC), a full-service instructional and consultative "academy" for business-owners and managers. UBC offers nine levels of advanced intensive coursework and customized, on-site workshops, publishes the Universal Business Consultant Newsletter (UBCN) for subscribing alumni, and currently has offices in Los Angeles, London, Honolulu, and Hong Kong.

As a long-time consultant and instructor of middle-middle and upper-middle-managers in the Los Angeles metropolitan area, I've seen my fair share of problems. But no manager is ever beyond help. As I gaze back on my years, the number one problem that sticks out in my mind about my business is weak managers. If "weak manager" appeared in the Webster's Dictionary, I have a feeling it would be defined as one who rarely or only inconsistently applies adequate force behind his managerial hand. In my advanced courses as well as in my publications I emphasize a set of lessons that are easy to learn and even easier to apply.

First of all, the manager must learn to use coercion effectively. Coercion might sound like a dirty word, but consider its usefulness to managers the world over. Fundamentally, coercion's purpose is to induce psychological regression in an employee by bringing a superior force from outside to bear on his will to resist, resulting in a more effective managerial style. Regression of this sort is basically a controlled loss of autonomy and is marked by the return to an earlier behavioral level. As an employee regresses, his learned personality traits fall away in reverse chronological order. Destructive capacities such as ironic detachment or a regard for one's self are lost. With practice, an employee + coercion will = a worker.

Always remember that an employee's sense of identity depends on continuity in his surroundings, habits, appearance, relations with others, etc. Always remember, too, the four C's of good managing: Careful Coercion Corrodes Continuity. An example: an employee's desk is an extension of his body, and the manager should look closely at its artifacts for hints at the

Check. But what is Service exactly?

To begin with, Mr. Man, I'm informed of the quarterly Blood Drive/Pancake Breakfast—a word combination generating a slew of disturbing mental images. Nevertheless, the Rotarians are said to have collected more than 7,450 pints of fine Oak Forest hemoglobin since 1976. Equally impressive is the ten thousand dollars collected for Rotary International's Polio Plus program, a project dedicated to nothing less than wiping polio from the face of the earth by Rotary's centennial in 2005. Oak Forest Rotary has also developed their "Books for Zimbabwe" project, vowing to collect twenty thousand schoolbooks for that country's supply-poor rural schools. Not earthshaking projects on the level of the United Way, nor flashy contributions to the "tear down the system" method of social reform, I suppose, but nice attempts to make a dent in a weary world.

On the other hand, is the path to world peace truly paved with pancakes? And why pancakes, fer God's sake? On the face of it, they lend themselves to high volume and returns at low investment. From a semiotics angle, they're squishy, boneless things, capable of offending no one. Conversely, what sort of communistic, un-American monster doesn't like pancakes? After experiencing this momentary thumb wrestling of conscience, I decide that flapjack purveying for the common good is guileless enough. Girl Scouts peddle cookies, Scientologists hawk galvanometers, and Rotarians hold pancake breakfasts. A tradition is a tradition, and a buck is a buck.

The meeting moves on to the featured speaker. Babbitt suffered through the gobbledygook of the American New Thought League. We get the Nineties equivalent: Chuck, who will discuss the many, many, many uses of the Internet. Crewcutted Chuck (who I suspect works from his subbasement, to judge by his laserwritten business cards), drones on about "Web sites," "hits," "search engines," and other buzzwords gleaned from back issues of PC World, while competing with tinkling piano and crowd noises trickling in from the main room. Tellingly, young Rotarian John is rapt, while éminence grise Hugh chooses instead to nibble at his seasoned fries.

After an interminable half hour, during which the Rotarians slide down in their chairs like overheated tree sloths, Chuck wraps it up by remarking how dandy the Web is for small businesses.

Suddenly shaken from their collective languor, the re-energized Rotarians bolt up from their seats and out the door in a vote of no-confidence against poor Chuck. Sorry, Chuck, no time to dither; they've got buses to manage, eyes to examine, and retirements to savor. Fifteen escaped Rotarians too late, President Rich strikes the bell and announces, "Dismissed."

Sitting nearby, my father grins.

"Yeah, that ought to do it, Rich," he gibes.

"We Build"

ON May 20, 1998, the Oak Forest Kiwanis Club broke my stony heart. Arriving at noon, again, at the House of Hughes, again, I ask the hostess where the Kiwanians are meeting. Around the corner, I am told, and heading in that direction I enter a large room bursting with golden citizens, each head marked with shades of silver and grey, or liver-spotted skin. One table is a virtual gynogerontocracy, populated by little old ladies noshing upon tuna melts. I make the false assumption that this is the Kiwanis table, and walk toward it until a patch-covered banner catches my eye.

Kiwanis International has 300,000 members. Two of them are sitting at a table against the back wall. House of Hughes house rules decree that a club must have twenty-five members in order to use the "private" room. Rotary has twenty-five; Kiwanis does not, and holds court in the main room instead.

Retiree husband and wife members Chet and Sandy greet me readily, informing me that my contact Ralph—a Rotarian, a Kiwanian, and a Promise Keeper (!) all in one—has yet to arrive. Shortly thereafter Ralph keeps his promise and shows up, offering, to my relief, a firm handshake rather than a manly hug. After him comes Linda, who at thirty-eight is thirty years younger than the next youngest Kiwanian. That makes four. Our greetings out of the way, we sit down and order lunch. I find I have a serious yen for a tuna melt.

Today's main order of business is the club's dissolution. Kiwanis International bylaws stipulate that no

weakest part of that body. Pictures of children and loved ones might point to the family. Postcards from last summer's vacation point to the importance of leisure. Stuffed animals surely signify a need to be hugged, even loved. Managers, make careful note of these observations.

Disrupting an employee's continuity can always be a productive method of applying managerial pressure. Detention and a deprivation of sensory stimuli are two methods which on the surface sound draconian, but which, on second look, are easily adapted for the workplace. Detention can mean arriving early and staying late. Contrive ways to keep an employee by your side all day, perhaps by making appointments with the employee early in the morning and around 4 p.m., when "quitting time-itis" has been known to set in. Depriving sensory stimuli can be accomplished with embarrassing ease: take away an employee's radio.

I have been suggesting some possible actions for the weak manager. In some cases, perhaps only the *threat* of action is enough. I always tell the managers in my courses to internalize the difference between threats suggested and threats enacted. Remember a rule I call, "Follow through is up to you." The threat of coercion usually weakens or destroys resistance more effectively than coercion itself.

Just as an example—the threat to inflict pain can trigger fears far more damaging than the immediate sensation of pain. And sometimes pain causes a sense of hopelessness, nihilism, and despair that is too bleak even to be useful to managers who are experts in these techniques. A reminder: this example has nothing to do with actual conduct in the workplace.

On the subject of coercion, I would be remiss if I didn't mention my experience with hypnosis. I have had some indescribable personal success with the hypnotic arts. Though it's true that answers obtained from an employee under the influence of hypnotism are highly suspect, as they are often based upon the suggestions of the manager and are distorted or fabricated, hypnosis does have its clear benefits and I remain one of its vocal champions.

An employee's strong desire to escape the stress of the situation can create a state of mind called "heightened suggestibility." The manager can then take advantage of this state of mind by creating a situation in which an employee will cooperate because he *believes* he has been hypnotized. This hypnotic situation can be created using a magic room technique.

For example, imagine that an employee is given a hypnotic suggestion that his hand is growing warm. In the magic room, his hand actually does become warm, with the aid of a bi-level, rheostat-controlled diathermy machine previously concealed in the arm of the special office chair. An employee may be given a suggestion that a cigarette will taste bitter and then be given a cigarette prepared to have a slight but noticeably bitter taste.

In view of the litigious nature of U.S. society today, being a business owner and an employer of people has never been more difficult. The bad news is it probably won't get easier. The good news is that there are things you can do, as a manager or business owner, that you probably haven't tried yet.

While there is no drug that can force every employee to divulge all the information he has, in a state of heightened suggestibility and in a duly-outfitted magic room, a harmless sugar pill can have extraordinary effects. The manager can tell an employee that the placebo is a truth serum that will make him want to talk and prevent all his lying. Things grow complicated here and can fast become overheated, psychologically speaking, but the end result

club shall fall below twenty members. At their zenith, the Oak Forest Kiwanians had eighteen. Kiwanis let it slide, but now that membership has dwindled to a scant seven, the pressure is on. Death, apathy, and plain and simple lapsing have struck hard. Chet tells me that one very active member died recently, another moved, and two others have risen to positions in state government. The remainder are content to leave membership to check-writing duty. Although a passionate core remains in Oak Forest, Kiwanis International is putting the screws on the club to close shop. Before my eyes they do just that. Ralph reads off the few mail-in votes, all two in favor of disbanding. Chet, Sandy, Ralph, and Linda give their votes as well, and with Band-Aid removal quickness, it's over.

If the Oak Forest Kiwanians are disbanding, it's not for lack of trying. The usual potential membership hives were approached: city hall, the police and fire departments, the library—all reacting with a fervor usually reserved for laundry day. Attempts were made at hometown boosterism by holding meetings solely at Oak Forest eateries, including the New Horizon, Chin's, and the swanky Oak Forest Buffet. "We were most successful when we met there," Chet wistfully recalls. "We had our own room." Finally, they settled on the House of Hughes, regrettably located in Crestwood, a suburb that manages to be even more nondescript than Oak Forest. So here we are, conducting a meeting for a club that no longer exists in a city it does not represent. Not exactly Kafka, but a wee bit bleak.

With nothing else to do but talk, I ask the usual questions, starting with what do . . . sorry, what *did* you do exactly? For their smallish size and brief tenure, the Kiwanians did quite a bit.

Following the Kiwanis International party line, the Oak Forest Kiwanians made "Young Children: Priority One." "If the Lions were for glasses, Kiwanis is for young children between the ages of one and five," Chet explains. Yes, yet another extremely safe and utterly unimpeachable goal. Well, not everyone sees distributing hypo needles and condoms as the best solutions, I guess.

As Rotary annexed polio, so Kiwanis adopted IDD (iodine deficiency disorder) as their disease of choice. IDD is just another archaic medical condition in our hemisphere, owing to our ingestion of iodized salt. Regrettably, IDD continues to expand goiters and induce mental and physical retardation in poor children worldwide. Kiwanis International is going Rotary one better by vowing to wipe out *their* disease before A.D. 2000. Oak Forest Kiwanis Club fought the good fight, and collected from $1,200 to $1,800 for IDD over the past six years. They've also raised funds for local school reading programs; "Together We Cope," a charity providing needy folks with food, clothing, and whatnot; and the Crippled Children's Camp in Plymouth, Indiana.

Come again?

I heard it right: Crippled Children's Camp. How utterly Dickensian. Of course it's a "Crippled Children's Camp"; "Camp Gimpy" would be inappropriate. A decision is made to donate the remainder of the club's funds to the camp.

If you're wondering where all the money comes from, it boils down to two carbohydrate-laden staples: peanuts and spaghetti. By way of explanation, it's really only the fourth Friday of September when Kiwanians prowl the streets, hawking tiny bags of peanuts, not every damn time you turn around. Another popular fund-raiser was the annual Candlelight Bowl, where participants binged on a "nice dinner," then bowled a couple of frames. Kindly don't laugh. This is the extent of Oak Forest nightlife. Besides, upwards of ninety people showed up, raising more than one thousand dollars for IDD, crippled children, and the like.

I ask my other big question: With such impeccable credentials, why aren't more people donning the Kiwanis garrison cap?

Quietly outspoken Chet minces no words: "These are aging clubs." Ralph, Sandy, and Linda nod in sad agreement, also pointing out that time, or the lack thereof, remains the biggest obstacle. Most suburban retirees these days are too busy enjoying their golden years, traveling and so forth, while younger people are raising families, with Dad playing a bigger role in bringing up the kids. Second careers are becoming the norm in places like Oak Forest, and while many would like to help out, according to Linda, "It's faster to hand over a check than to give up your time."

is that an employee will indeed talk, as it's clearly his only avenue of escape from a depressing situation. He will want to believe that he has been drugged because then nobody can blame him for telling his entire story. A mere sugar pill provides him with the rationalization he needs to cooperate. The manager will keep a number of these sugar pills handy.

I have mentioned some of the more powerful techniques used to create a useful state of regression. Sometimes, however, the manager should consider more subtle means, such as:

—Manipulating time
—Retarding and advancing clocks
—Offering free meals at odd times
—Disrupting sleep schedules with either early morning or late night "emergency" calls
—Unpatterned and aimless questioning sessions
—Vigorous nonsensical questioning
—Ignoring halfhearted attempts to cooperate
—Rewarding noncooperation
—Arbitrary body language

Surely I have suggested that there remains a wide and plentiful universe of options available to the manager who possesses an open mind.

Members of the "Bowling Alone" hysteria club may see Robert Putnam's dreaded decay of civic engagement in the club's apparent stagnation. I disagree. The question isn't one of willingness to serve, but of relevance. The clubs are perceived as being, not to mince words, quaint. Much like today's grade-schoolers' choice between joining Boy/Girl Scouts or tae kwon do, when it's a choice between learning how to tie a sheepshank or splintering boards with your fists, it's no contest. Another particularly galling coffin nail, according to Chet, is the inexplicable insistence of some clubs on remaining exclusively male, despite Kiwanis International's bold decision to go coed way back in 1987. Ralph further notes that, once upon a time, Uncle Sam allowed employers a tax deduction when they paid part of an employee's club dues. Not anymore.

So why did these Kiwanians stick it out? Ralph answers, using a rather embarrassing word. "I've always been a joiner," he says, laying his Babbitt card squarely on the table. "I've always believed that if you choose to live in a place, you should want to make it desirable."

"Some people join thinking, 'If I join, it should help my business prospects.' That's not a good thing," Chet interjects without a trace of guile. "A sense of altruism should be the best reason."

Despite all my ingrained cynicism, I believe them. The world, however, remains unimpressed, and the Oak Forest Kiwanis Club disintegrates into good intentions and fairy dust. The meeting ends with the members agreeing to defect to the club in nearby Tinley Park. The dissolution is made manifest when the club's call-to-order bell is dragged out—a dinged and melancholy thing whose brass Kiwanis logo has snapped off. The Kiwanians are not sure what to do with the threadbare American flag.

"The poor thing's seen better days, hasn't it?" Sandy says.

Oh, stop your post-Watergate tittering, you heartless bastards.

"We Serve"

THE Oak Forest Lions Club is long dead; the Oak Forest Chamber of Commerce tells me so. The only remnant of the club is a rust-spattered sign standing near the city-limit signpost at 143rd and Central. Curiously, or perhaps not so curiously, Lions Club remains the largest of all the clubs, with 1.4 million members and 43,000 clubs across the globe. When one considers what the clubs once were, however, the phrase "That and a quarter . . ." suggests itself.

Yet, while the service clubs themselves continue to drift and fragment away from their illusory small town roots, the "International" club corporations behind them plug along, allocating funds to worthy causes, peddling club logo-embossed fountain pens and golf equipment through their catalogs, and seeking out new avenues of boosterism in Third World and former Eastern Bloc countries.

Despite the reader's expectations, I will not close with a smart-assed remark. On the contrary, I laud the clubs for outliving the fashionable sneers leveled at them. I congratulate them for never pretending to be havens for individualism in the first place, and for providing otherwise clueless burghers with a smattering of a sense of civic responsibility. I applaud them for organizing for no grislier purpose than scratching one another's backs, and occasionally lending an overweening hand to the "poor unfortunates" of the world. Most of all, I praise to the heavens their utter, ineluctable squareness, their refusal to accommodate a younger, hipper audience. Such purity of vision is to be cherished, but whether for its pleasantly ersatz compassion or its bovine complacency, I'll leave for the reader to decide.

EXCERPTS FROM THE TINLEY PARK POLICE NEIGHBORHOOD WATCH NEWSLETTER, MAY 1998

The Pines

6300 block Pine Ridge   5-5   1:50 PM
Report of theft of fireplace from house under construction, case under investigation.

181st St. & 66th Ave.   5-5   5:26 PM
Report of male white subject in brown car that just shot a paint ball at resident's vehicle. Officer will attempt to make contact with offender who was identified later this evening.

6300 block of 181st St.   5-5   7:01 PM
Police dispatch received 911 call from 8 year old boy stating is a stranger at door, babysitter in bathroom. Mom came home while child on phone, no problem, was a neighbor.

18000 block 66th Ave.   5-13   12:55 PM
Resident stated she believes a known subject may be stalking her, drives a red Trans Am.

17900 block 66th Ct.   5-28   7:48 PM
Sometime between 7 pm on 5/20 and 7 pm this date persons unknown took lawn decoration from yard.

Oak Village

6600 block Pine Point   5-21   10:28 PM
Resident reported 2 large Flamingo plant holders were taken.

Barrett

17500 block 70th Ct.   5-21   6:57 AM
Resident reported theft of glider from front porch.

6800 block 177th St.   5-21   9:40 AM
Sometime between 8 pm on 5/20 and 9:30 am this date persons unknown took sundial from resident's front yard.

Edgewater

16700 block Lakewood   5-1   5:24 PM
Report of female in burgundy Chevy Camaro racing up and down street, squealing tires, pulled into parking lot, subject located, settled by officer.

Lake Bluff and Lakeside   5-17   3:59 PM
Subjects who do not live there on private property are fishing, are with people who live there.

Continued on page 84

Chapters of Eleven

KIM PHILLIPS-FEIN

A N hour before closing time, the Chicago Mercantile Exchange hardly seems like a dignified institution at the epicenter of American finance: It's more like a sports bar. Throngs of grownup frat-boy traders stare at numbers flashing on a gigantic screen. Moments of calm alternate with paroxysms of activity, as the *Animal House* lookalikes pump their fists into the air and gesticulate like manic umpires to the callers ringing the pit. Pieces of paper fly through the air, deftly handled by college-age runners wearing the baggy gold jackets of Team Merc. Abstract pork bellies and livestock—and the abstractions of abstractions, stock indexes and interest rates—are furiously tossed back and forth in a never-ending game that seems always to be in the ninth inning.

Does bankruptcy ever enter the minds of the wild-eyed millionaires who bounce like cheerleaders in the panicked atmosphere of the pit? If so, they can forcibly expel the thought with a few adrenaline-fueled trades. But come October, the wizards at the Merc— alchemically spinning loss into

gold—won't be able to take their minds off going bust. That's when the Merc begins trading a brand new future index based on the quarterly number of bankruptcies. The Merc's new toy—the Quarterly Bankruptcy Index—will take the number of bankruptcies in the previous quarter as a baseline. Though the product may sound bizarre, it's supposed to function like insurance: The credit card companies stand to lose a small amount if bankruptcies fall, but they'll offset potentially great losses if bankruptcies rise. Peach farmers and hog merchants can buy futures to lower risk; why shouldn't banks, credit card companies, and department stores be able to use the derivatives market to offset their mounting losses to bankruptcy?

The notion of people getting rich betting on the spiraling number of bankruptcies may seem a little odd to rubes like you and me. But personal bankruptcies hit an all-time high in 1997, with more than 1.3 million people filing, and even more are expected to file in 1998; bank card companies claim to have lost between $10 and $12 billion as a result. Not that anyone should feel sorry for the credit industry, which borrows money at standard rates and lends it out at exorbitant ones. But, greedy bastards that they are, they're looking for some new financial tool to help insure themselves against loss—that is, when they aren't busy pressuring Congress to stiffen the penalties for bankruptcy. What makes the "deadbeat index" unusual is its casual nonchalance toward bankruptcy. While moralists vent public outrage over the spiraling number of bankruptcies, the master financial minds of the Merc have admitted the truth: Bankruptcy is normal today, an aspect of economic life to be insured against as though it were a fact of nature like drought or flood.

This routinization of bankruptcy is the polar opposite of the old Weberian version of economic behavior. The farmers and artisans of centuries ago felt a strict identity between self and pocketbook. Financial dealings were thought to reveal the most intimate truths about one's character. In the old pre-capitalist world, bankruptcy received the stiffest of punishments; the debtor relinquished freedom, property, and sometimes life itself. In England, bankruptcy was punishable by death through the eighteenth century; imprisonment for debt remained the norm until the days of Dickens. But advanced capitalist states have long since given up pushing business moralism to such extremes and have ceased to equate financial death with the real thing. Nineteenth-century re-

formers were horrified by the cruelty of debtor's prisons, but they were also disturbed by the fact that their own bourgeois peers could be thrown willy-nilly into the bin simply for making a bad deal or two right before a recession. As our contemporary economists might say, an economy built on rewarding risk can't afford to mete out too-harsh punishment for daredevil entrepreneurs whose stunts occasionally leave them lying bruised on the ground.

During the last fifty years, though, bankruptcy has been democratized. Today it's a condition that might be faced by anyone, not just entrepreneurs. And while the spending binges that land us in bankruptcy are hardly deeds of heroic capitalist risk-taking, they are far more important in reality to our larger economic well-being.

Nonetheless, this latest phase in the development of bankruptcy has brought loud public calls for a revival of the old pre-capitalist horror toward debt. Credit industry hacks and their minions on the Hill have taken up the mantle of personal responsibility, and have sought to transform the Nanny State into the Daddy State, a stern Federal superego that will scold debtors along with pregnant teens, divorcees, and other bearers of bad values. "Bankruptcy has become like a carwash. People go in, spend a little time inside and come out spotless," laments Mallory Duncan of the National Retail Federation, apparently longing for the days of public stocks and debtor's prison. "Bank-

ruptcy is becoming a financial strategy for too many Americans," moans Donald Ogilvie, executive vice president of the American Bankers Association, in a letter to *The Wall Street Journal*. "There are a whole lot of child-like adults with adult-like credit lines," keens Ronald Utt, senior fellow at the Heritage Foundation. But the ain't-it-awful crowd, hearkening back to yesteryear's business moralism, blithely ignores what the Merc cannily admits. Bankruptcy is a crucial safety valve for an economy that depends on mass consumption *and* low wages.

If the real cause of the rising number of bankruptcies was some sudden erosion of moral fiber, it would be testament to the malleability of the human spirit. In fact, we really don't need to juice up our econometric model with a virtue variable to see what has caused the rise in bankruptcies. As it turns out the change has fairly mundane origins: Bankruptcy is closely correlated with the ratio of debt to income, which has been rising rapidly ever since real wages stopped rising in the early Seventies. In other words, as people began to borrow to make up for stagnant wages, bankruptcies started to rise.

It's commonplace to blame the rise in bankruptcies on the new bankruptcy code, which, starting in late 1979, made it easier to discharge credit card debt. But bankruptcies had actually been climbing throughout the Seventies, from 173,000 personal and business bankruptcies in 1973 to 254,000 in 1975, before falling slightly to

226,000 in 1979. During these years, bankruptcy law didn't change, but consumer indebtedness did: Between 1973 and 1979 the ratio of total household debt to total household income rose from 58.6 percent to 64 percent. After the new law took effect, it's true, personal bankruptcies rose by 100,000, but the law was more a response to the bankruptcy trend than a cause.

The debt-income ratio rose steadily through the Eighties and Nineties, reaching 83.4 percent of household income in 1994; by 1997 debt service payments reached a shocking 16 percent of total household income. Credit card use climbed especially sharply during the Eighties and the Nineties. Between 1984 and the present, revolving credit (short-term debt, mainly credit cards) has more than tripled. And with rising debt, bankruptcies have rocketed, climbing from about 300,000 a year in the early Eighties to more than one million in 1996. This year it seems that once again a record number of people will file— more than 1.4 million.

This mountain of new debt may seem a sure sign of a country headed for the poorhouse. But in fact, the seemingly exorbitant amount of consumer debt is in large part responsible for the prosperity we've enjoyed these past few years. The Nineties expansion, in contrast to the Keynesian expansion of the Sixties, is fueled by consumption; consumption has averaged 67.8 percent of GDP in the Nineties, a higher proportion than during any other expansion since World War II.

Debt explains the otherwise mysterious appearance of a consumption-driven boom at a time when real wages have been falling or stagnant. The fact that the debt-to-income ratio has been climbing since 1973—the postwar peak for real wages—suggests that families have taken on debt in order to compensate for slow wage increases. Today, credit-driven spending is at historic levels, accounting for about 29 percent of the growth in consumption in the expansion that commenced in 1991. Today's credit explosion makes *The Bonfire of the Vanities* look sober; during the Eighties, credit accounted for just 23 percent of growth in consumption. From the standpoint of economic growth, there's no doubt the handy income supplement made possible by debt has been a lifesaver. But the corollary is a much larger number of bankruptcies, since stagnant wages and rising debt together mean that at some point people— well, lots of people—are inevitably going to default.*

Debt also has ideological benefits. By putting purchasing power into the hands of the vast majority without increased wages, it creates a fiction of social equality and sustains mass purchasing power even as income inequality widens. A million-odd bankruptcies is a small price to pay for such a handy illusion. Without the cushion of widely available credit, we'd risk a broad economic contraction, not to mention a whole lot of demands for higher wages. Rising profits, meager wage growth, and

---

* GDP figures are from Doug Henwood's Bureau of Economic Analysis database; figures on the proportion of growth in consumption financed by credit are calculated using his flow-of-funds database.

manic consumption are what drives the Nineties boom. Someone's gotta pay—and for the time being, the bill's going to Visa.

But who are the debtors who have been so much in the news of late? Are they the bearers of a new strain of shortsighted selfishness? Actually, they are more or less a cross section of the middle class. In occupational makeup, they mirror the country as a whole, but their incomes are far lower, and their debts far higher, than the general population. Median family income for bankruptcy petitioners in 1991 was $18,000—half the national average—and almost 30 percent of debtors had incomes below the poverty line. Debtors often owed one-and-a-half times their yearly income in short-term debt.

What these numbers suggest is that bankruptcy is now a routine part of middle-class American life. People borrow heavily, especially during expansions, when they expect—perhaps irrationally—that they'll be able to pay back all their debt. But should a single crisis befall a heavily indebted household, it's easy for it to fall hopelessly behind. Much of the rise in bankruptcies has occurred during economic upswings, which puzzles pundits, though it may not be so complex: In good times banks are willing to lend, credit card companies hawk their wares, and people are lulled into a false sense of economic security. But when disaster hits they topple right away: More than half of 1991 bankrupts reported interrupted employment in the two years

before they filed. Forty percent of older bankrupts faltered under heavy medical debt. Many are single parents. Their commonalities are not immorality but a brush with a single financial disaster—divorce, layoff, catastrophic heart attack—which is all it takes to send a debt-ridden family's finances up in flames. So an extremely high bankruptcy rate is pretty much to be expected in a society with scant social welfare provisions, stagnant wages, easy credit, and a high cultural premium on status-through-consumption. You may have lost your middle-class salary; you may not have the job security of a degree or a union. But your debt is as good as anyone else's.*

Calvin.

But for other debtors, the rude disruption of their middle-class lifestyles hasn't been the result of sudden disaster; it's been mere pretense from the start. These are spenders who aren't weighed down by a rare big-ticket item but who bankrupt themselves with spending sprees totally out of keeping with their incomes. Poor people are the credit industry's growth sector; between 1977 and 1989 the proportion of households earning between $10,000 and $20,000 who have at least one credit card rose from 33 percent in 1983 to 44 percent in 1995, according to Federal Reserve economist Peter Yoo. Even among households with in-

comes under $10,000, 32 percent owned credit cards in 1995. Lower-income households also use their cards more heavily than they used to. (Although wealthy households still account for the majority of credit card debt, average credit card debt for households in the lower half of the income distribution increased at a 14 percent annual rate between 1992 and 1995, compared to an 8 percent annual rate for households in the top half of the income distribution.)

For poorer families, debt is an irresistible supplement to low incomes. I went to Chicago's federal bankruptcy court and looked through some of the petitioners' files. Among them I found Mary B., a middle-aged woman, married with no children. She's worked at the National School Towel Service for sixteen years; her annual salary is $12,000. She will probably never buy a home or get a degree. Nonetheless, she declared bankruptcy in April 1998, after running up credit card bills of $9,200. According to court documents, she charged $5,300 of "ordinary household goods and supplies" to her Discover Card, and $3,200 more to her First Chicago card. Let's reflect on what these might be: a trip to Sears for a new washer-dryer? A jaunt to Marshall Field's, perhaps for a cute pair of earrings and a chi-chi black dress? Marie Anne T.'s files tell a similarly ordinary story. A nurse technician for

---

* Financial profiles of petitioners from "Consumer Debtors Ten Years Later: A Financial Comparison of Consumer Bankrupts, 1981-1991," by Theresa Sullivan, Elizabeth Warren and Jay Westbrook, *American Bankruptcy Journal*, Spring 1994. Also see "Consumer Bankruptcy: Issues Summary," by Elizabeth Warren of Harvard Law School.

five years, earning a salary of $18,000, this single mother with two young adult children managed to ring up bills of $13,700 on her credit cards in 1997, increasing her disposable income by 76 percent and making stops at Sears (for a new lawn mower and stereo, according to court files) and at Montgomery Ward (new tires for the car?). She also owed $46,000 in secured debt, mostly for no fewer than three automobiles, shared with her children. Neither Mary nor Marie Anne could realistically have had hoped to pay back her exorbitant bills, no matter how bountiful the economy seemed. Instead, each one simply "passed" as middle class for a year, flaunting her new clothes and household goods.

Lénine.

There's an odd poetic justice in the bankruptcies of Mary and Marie Anne. Banks and credit companies are, strictly speaking, the direct source of their illusory "income." But considered more abstractly, it is their bosses who are lending them money. Most households are net debtors, while only the very richest are net creditors. In an overall sense, in other words, the working classes are forever borrowing from their employers. Lending replaces decent wages, masking income disparities even while aggravating them through staggering interest rates. If Mary's wages were higher, she might not have needed those credit cards—and, of course, her boss wouldn't have quite so much money lying around to lend. Credit and bankruptcy can sometimes even seem like class warfare by other means: Mary and Marie Anne are simply treating themselves to a long-delayed raise.

But there is also something tragic about quick bankruptcy and easy credit, about the buying frenzies of folks like Mary and Marie Anne or their wealthier counterparts who are laid low by exclusive summer camps, music lessons, and private schools. Bankruptcy may provide short-term relief for consumers locked into endless debt servicing, but it can't deliver on the promise of sunny days and blue skies held out by the lawyers shilling on late-night TV. Upper-class moralists may gnash their teeth, but bankruptcy serves their interests fairly well: By obscuring collective problems, credit provides easy individual escapes into a world where everything can be yours. Frustration with empty, boring work, a stagnant salary, and the tedium of making ends meet can be expressed as the craving for a waffle iron, a piece of lingerie, a bright plastic toy for the kid. Bankruptcy transforms the nasty crunch confronting the middle class—"downsizing," rising housing prices, slow real income growth, attacks on unions—into an individual morality play of desire, gluttony, confession, and finally redemption, as the forgiven debtor goes out to borrow once again.

X-TREME teambuilders

"A mind stretched by a new experience can never go back to its old dimensions."
–Oliver Wendell Holmes

Do you believe that adventure-learning is the best way to build a motivated, highly effective management team? Then why send your company's managers parachuting or bungee-jumping like everybody else? Get the edge on the competition with X-TREME TEAMBUILDERS: We "go deep" with our unique adventure-learning packages. *Your company will never be the same again.*

Learning from Experience

The best teams are not accidental.
They are created through hard work, synergy, and adherence to strategic vision. We believe that:
• Success is captured by individuals who go beyond their limitations.
• Ordinary people are capable of more than they believe—much more.
• Personal adversity is the most powerful teaching tool.
In a transformative adventure-learning environment that fosters positive risk-taking and intense lateral collaboration, X-TREME TEAMBUILDERS will help the members of your management team acquire the tools they need to survive, individually and professionally.

The team-building adventure described in this brochure is just *one* of the *many* experiential-learning options available through our company. In each one, your management team's members will have many opportunities to experiment with different behaviors and attitudes, learning from the direct consequences of their actions. They will then return to the workplace with new, more effective options for action.

Our most popular adventure-learning package is the Deliverance trip, which offers a progression of adventure and experiential learning opportunities, done in the greatest teaching laboratory of all: the nearly inaccessible Cahulawassee River, guarded by the deep woods near Aintry, Georgia.

Your first challenge: Negotiate with threatening hillbillies over the price of driving your sport utility vehicles to a pre-designated site at the river's end. Learn to embrace and transform the negative energy of resistance, which forward-thinking companies often face. Banjo serenade by ominously silent local optional.

"You don't beat it. You don't beat this river."
—Taylor Fuller, Senior Vice President, Datacom Inc.

"There's something in the woods and the water that we have lost in the city"
—Kevin Fitzgibbon, Quality Assurance Manager, Old Navy Inc.

On the first leg of your two-night trip enjoy canoeing on exciting but manageable rapids, fish for your supper with a bow and arrow, and sleep under the dark blanket of night only the deep woods can provide. An excellent opportunity for meditative reprioritization.

"Machines are gonna fail, and the system's gonna fail. And then, survival. That's the game: Survive!"
—Drew Nevin, Director of Overseas Operations, KFC

Through power risk-taking, your team will learn to resolve ethical dilemmas effectively. Now begins the important work of consensus-building, improvising real-life solutions using tools provided by your own ingenuity.

"Each exercise has a real life application. Pulling together, planning and working together, allows common people to produce uncommon results."
—Brent Powell, Vice President of Engineering, Unistress Inc.

"I kept repeating, 'I can't do this, I'm afraid to do this.' But with a great deal of encouragement from my teammates, I did do this!"
—Todd "Choppy" Andersen, Corporate Counsel, Bank One

On day two it's time for some invasive mentoring, as your team gets divided into two mutually accountable sub-teams. One sub-team will undergo radical boundary redefinitions (no extra equipment needed)—requiring the other group to move into high-pressure problem solving mode.

Bound together now as a focused and fearless group, you haven't received your money's worth yet! Get ready to shoot off the learning curve as you face opportunites for stress-management and thinking outside the box that include: going into shock, being shot at by vengeful hillbillies, and even losing your identity.

"Sometimes you have to lose yourself before you can find anything."
—Blake Eggers, Vice President, R&D, H. J. Heinz Co.

What happens when the weakest member of your team has to scale a cliff, kill a man, and lower his body to the ground-team below? You'll all learn that individual peak experiences can't be separated from aggressive cooperation.

Your final challenge: Transgressive adherence to a mutually-arrived-at strategic vision. Provide a convincing and effective cover story to local authorities or face serious jail-time.

"The single most impactful concept that came into play was that the goals that require more than one person are the accomplishments most worth achieving"
—Gordy Lawrence, Director of Public Relations, Bronson Canyon Entertainment

"It was just like Chip said, the whole program was facilitated with our needs in mind! I can't wait to get back to work and translate my personal peak experience into real-life problem-solving with what's left of my team!"
—Harrison Gould, Browser Evangelist, Lycos, Inc.

Text: Josh Glenn and A.S. Hamrah. Art: Jessica Abel

Saturday Night at the Movies

MARSHMALLOWS. I see the marshmallows. They fling themselves above me, high flyin'. I watch them with a dulled absorption.

Patting. Something is patting my face. A gentle rain of gentle pats. On my nose, cheeks and mouth.

Then God speaks. God is the atmosphere in which marshmallows fling themselves toward the heavens. And God is the moral climate in which one's face is patted. But God is also capable of infusing his world with voice.

God can say: "Butch, what in the hell are you doing?"

My father-who-art-on-the-couch, hallowed be thy Life-on-TV. He hath risen like Christ from the tomb; he is a lily sprouting like a mushroom from the humid cushions of the davenport. He has lifted himself from recumbency, as if someone had asked the famous reclining Buddha for a dance.

So I'm looking straight up out of my own sympathetic grave. My father is on his knees looking back over the edge of the chesterfield, as if over the edge of his own coffin.

His arms rest on the edge, God brooding over his world, wondering, "Why did I make *that*?" I lie below him, on the floor, flat on my back, dozens of Kraft miniature marshmallows littered around my head like spent shrapnel.

"I'm not doin' nothin', Dad."

"No, Son, that's not nothin'. I can only wish you were doin' nothin'. Nothin' would be a big step up from this. Compared to this, nothin' gets your name on a banner high up in the rafters of the high school gymnasium. So, no, it's not nothin'. It's the quality of the *somethin'* that I'm wondering about."

I scrunch my face searching for a way of expressing my sense of hopeless bewilderment.

"No, Son, let me tell you what you're doin'. You're throwing marshmallows up in the air and letting them land on your face. Can you give me the rhyme and reason for this?"

I can feel my eyebrows, nose, and mouth shudder and convulse. What have I meant?

God clucks his tongue. "You just don't make sense."

"Saturday Night at the Movies" is excerpted from *Memories of My Father Watching TV* (Dalkey Archive Press, 1998). The author wishes to acknowledge the samples taken from Paul Driver's "A Third Man Cento," in *Sight and Sound*, Winter 1989/90.

He continues. "Now let's take a look at what your hands are doing."

My hands. Again. Doing things. Why were boys supposed to be responsible for what their little hands did? It wasn't fair. I looked over at my right hand, fearing the worst. Marshmallows had, over a period of tremendous geological change, of the complete collapse of one climate empire after another, marshmallows had, I may now safely reveal, now that it is too late and no amount of filtering, recycling, and federal intervention will make the least difference, marshmallows had with the persistent force that is nature's own, melted down between my fingers, dripped through like stalactites or mites, making thus a most guilty and sticky clotted cream.

"Not that hand. The other hand."

Oh, that hand was an innocent hand! Let me look then for the true culprit, mister left hand, mister sneaky sinister. But I couldn't find it.

"Where is it, Dad?"

"Where's what?"

"My other hand."

"Where's your other hand? You can't find your own hand? Jesus! Send out a fucking search party! Call the FBI! He can't find his own goddamn hand!"

He waited. I did nothing. Then with a mocking look of exasperation he held his own left hand out as if to show me how it was done. With his extended left hand he formed a pistol. With the pistol he touched his temple.

I turned my head to the left and was suddenly looking right down the barrel. I could see the whorling bore of the gun, so much like a fingerprint.

Using my sodden right hand, I gently and compassionately lowered my rigid left, just praying that it was no hair-trigger affair. A tragedy averted.

Then Dad turned and sat back down on the davenport. Over the edge I could just see his hand gesture as though he were trying to throw a curveball, which I took to mean I should come sit with him.

Now this may all seem like just another evening in your average, damaged middle-class household. Not so! Remember, my father had not spoken to me since I was an infant. This was like wanting to know who had killed your best friend and then being given the extraordinary opportunity to ask questions of the victim himself.

I got up from behind the couch, wiping my fingers on my blue jeans, and sat next to my father. I kept my hands on my lap where I could keep an eye on them. Before us, like a dumb show, were my sisters. Winny moved to-and-fro before the TV like a deranged shuttle. Janey stood to the right, her mouth open like an orator's. A deep "Oh" emerged from her.

My father considered them. "Jesus Christ. As if you weren't bad enough. What in the world are your sisters doing?"

"I don't know."

"Are they always like this?"

"Maybe."

"What do you know?"

"I don't know."

At this point, of course, anybody's fatherly despair would be in order. But at just that moment I realized what a once-in-a-lifetime opportunity stood before me. I was speaking with my father. We were having a chat. I could ask him a question if I dared. I could ask him, what happened? Who dunnit? Were there witnesses? Where might my mighty revenge focus its awful energy? Time became mythic.

"Dad."

"Yes, Son."

"Can I ask you a question?"

"Sure."

"Are you happy?"

"Am I happy?"

"Yeah."

"Yes, I'm a very happy person."

"You are?"

"Of course."

"How do you know?"

"I'm happy because I just am. I have your mother and I have you kids and we have Poochie and the house and nice things like the TV."

"Dad, why do you watch TV every night?"

"I like the TV, Son. I enjoy it. It's very entertaining."

"You watch TV because it's entertaining?"

"That's right."

"Oh."

(Pause)

"Dad, why don't you talk to me or Winny or Janey?"

"I don't have anything to say to you. It's nothing personal. If I had something to say, I'd say it."

"Well, why don't you have something to say?"

"Like what?"

"Like anything."

"Like now?"

"I guess so. Yeah. We're talking now. Why can't we always do this?"

David Berman

"This is different because we're not really talking, we're talking about talking."

"Oh."

(Pause)

"Dad, why do you drink?"

"Drink?"

"You always drink that stuff that Mom calls booze. That Old Crow booze."

"Well, again, it's nothing mysterious. I just like to drink."

"You like to drink?"

"Yes. It makes me feel good. I enjoy it. It's part of what makes being an adult fun. When you grow up, you'll like to drink too. Drinking is like a good friend."

"Oh."

"So you see, Son, I'm happy because I have a nice TV to watch and drinks to drink. And that's all there is to it."

"Oh."

"Say, hey, listen, let's cut all this jabber and watch a movie. What do you say? It's Saturday night and there's a movie on. One of my favorites."

"What's the name of it?"

"The Third Man."

"What about Winny and Janey?"

"Leave them be. This movie's for you and me. Except Winny keeps getting in the way."

Dad gets up and moves Winny to one side. She continues to pace robot-like but out of our view.

"You make a better door than you do a window, Winny," he says.

"Son, have I ever told you about my experiences in postwar Vienna, when I was with the Allied Army of Occupation?"

Not a damned word.

"I never knew the old Vienna before the war, with its Strauss music, its glamour and easy charm—Constantinople suited me better."

"Constantiwhat?"

"Well, I had many fine adventures and I'm gonna tell you every one of them. But when Carol Reed and Orson Welles made this movie in Vienna back in 1948, they put me in it!"

"You're in this movie?"

"Bet your bottom dollar!"

"Who are you?"

"What makes you think I'm a who?"

"What else could you be?"

"Maybe I'm a building or a bridge."

"You're a bridge in this movie?"

"I'm kidding you, Son. Why don't you just watch and tell me if you think someone or something is me."

A black-and-white shadowy world begins to emerge. It is the world of my parents, the world before I was born.

A brisk cosmopolitan narrator speaks: *"Vienna doesn't look any worse than a lot of other European cities, bombed about a bit . . . Oh wait, I was going to tell you . . . about Holly Martins from America . . ."*

"Dad, you were from America!"

"Sure was."

"Well, is that you? Holly Martins?"

"Don't talk. Watch the movie, Son."

"He came all the way here to visit a friend of his. The name was Lime, Harry Lime."

Opening Credits: A striated field, like a ruled pad of paper, made of the strings of a zither. Immediately the strings begin to vibrate, resonate with their great theme. Harry Lime. Harry Lime! Everything in this world evokes him while he remains persistently hidden. But this zither, our first "authenticity" in a movie that is often like a documentary of Cold War Vienna, has its own peculiarities. Are zithers truly a Germanic instrument? Is this sunny sound not more appropriate to the Mediterranean? The Greek *kithara*. Think of Vienna, whose grim streets are like claustrophobic canyons. Its severe facades always seem just a degree away from toppling. Why is this music here? It plays a tune that is lilting in pure, deranged contradiction to its context. It is the joie-de-vivre-unto-death. It is possessed, demoniacal, happy-go-lucky, a real self-motivator, fatal, unhinged, a good chap, funny, misplaced, grimy, suicidal, scandalous, merry, jocund, fleeting, ditty-like, of a certain airiness, depraved, condemned, merciless, unrepentant, and in general a scandal. When *The Third Man* played on TV, during my childhood, there was no escaping this zither which seemed to drench the house in human tears. It is the most perfect and perfectly inappropriate music in the history of soundtracks. This theme will plague us throughout the movie like a madness whose only virtue is persistence: it will not be forgotten. Da da da da da da . . . da da. This is a false gaiety. This is laughing when things ain't funny.

Porter: "Sorry for the gravediggers. Hard work in this frost."

Vienna: "Bombed about a bit." *The Third Man* is about the postwar four-power occupation of Vienna. Most of the film's contemporary viewers considered it a fairly accurate portrayal of Vienna, both visually and emotionally. The film's director, Carol Reed, used the piles of rubble, bombed-out houses, narrow streets and maze-like sewers. Inadvertently, he documented not only the place and time, but the metaphysical process by which the dislocations of World War II moved the West from the modern to the postmodern. It is visually and morally not unlike a much later and expressly postmodern movie, *Blade*

Runner. Both are movies about a world of decay on top of which is the high-tech super-efficiency of the State. The police powers of occupied Vienna know with a cruel particularity what is the case personally and ideologically in every collapsed corner of the city. Information is for the first time depicted as more durable and more real than granite.

Martins: "I was going to stay with him but he died Thursday."
Mr. Crabbit: "Goodness that's awkward."

The Third Man: This title. Why is it so unsettling? There is you and I. Me and Dad. There is the familiar comfort of the dual. Reality and TV. But this movie is telling me that there is a third character, beyond my control, beyond my perception, mocking me. The third man is the closeted man. The man of whom no one may speak. It is taboo. He is there and not there. Unspeakable. He laughs from darkened recesses like the Shadow. (Isn't part of the perfection of Orson Welles as Harry Lime the resonance of Welles's earlier radio career as the Shadow?) Welles's figural entry in a darkened Viennese doorway trails ghosts in its wake.

The third man is our madness whispering to us, "Nothing is as it seems. Everything you think you know is false." The simplicity of this revelation is appalling. There is you and your father and then there is a third man! The third man is your real father. You want him, you want him to come forward, and yet you fear that if he does you will learn things you do not wish to know.

The Plot: Holly Martins, a simple American writer of westerns, comes to Vienna at the request of his boyhood friend and idol, Harry Lime. He discovers that Lime is dead. We follow Holly Martins's inept but dogged pursuit of the enigmatic "third man" who supposedly witnessed Lime's death, but who, as it turns out, is actually Lime himself. Along the way, Martins, played by Joseph Cotten, is assaulted by ever-more shocking revelations—that Lime may have been murdered, that Lime is actually alive, that Lime is a racketeer whose watered-down penicillin has crippled innumerable children. As Martins's investigation proceeds, he himself becomes increasingly at risk from Harry's gangster friends and perhaps even the police. Ironically, Martins's perseverance also does damage to innocent people around him: a porter, Sergeant Paine, and Harry himself are killed, all in the course of Martins's efforts to know the "true story." Worse yet, his investigation calls attention to Lime's girlfriend, Anna, with whom Holly has fallen in love. Now, because of Holly's inept presence, the Soviets are interested in her and her forged passport.

Colonel Calloway: "Death's at the bottom of everything, Martins. Leave death to the professionals."

Mozart Café: Baron Kurtz, one of Harry's friends who was at the scene of the "accident," has arranged to speak with Holly. He is a decadent Viennese straight out of the paintings of Klimt. (Because of the persistently canted camera angles, the film has a generally Expressionist feel. This is a world off-kilter. It is a world of dawning nausea.) Kurtz has a repulsive little dog and a repulsive homosexual relationship with Dr. Winkel ("Veenkel!"). But Baron Kurtz is also a "third man" because he is also Joseph Conrad's Kurtz. Is the conclusion one should draw from this that everybody is in hiding, even those in the open? Does everyone mask a "third" presence? Holly's pathetic third presence: the idealistic American hero, the "lone rider of Santa Fe." So this is a detective story about Holly who seeks the truth of the spritely dead by rummaging among the dried husks of the living. Is not the film's thesis then: All those who are alive are really dead (in the sense that they obscure their real selves)? And all those who are apparently dead are alive? Bizarrely, Anna's depressed comment, "I want to be dead too," indicates that she alone among these many characters is truly alive. She admits her falsity and is thus most true. (Holly: "Anything really wrong, Anna, with your papers?" Anna: "They're forged.")

Anna: "He said I laughed too much."

Casanova Club: Shots of Kurtz playing overripe melodies on his violin to an obscenely fat and ugly woman eating soup. A violent cynicism: the romantic and the oleagi-

nous. Popescu: "Everyone ought to go careful in Vienna." Loud, lunatic, sobbing zither music.

The Reichsbrücke Bridge: Popescu arranges a meeting on this bridge to plot the murder of the porter. Looking hard, I catch my first sight of Lime—big, burly, great-coated, his back to the camera. My childhood self looks quickly to my father, "You?" "No, no, no. Pay attention."

Holly and Anna looking at a photograph.
Martins: "Harry?"
Anna, smiling: "Yes. He moved his head, but the rest is good isn't it?"

Harry's Street: The porter, who was about to spill Lime's secret to Holly, has been murdered. Holly enters a snarling crowd to find out what happened. Little Hansl arouses the crowd with his shrieks of "Papa, Papa." His childish words and gestures somehow imply that Martins is responsible. He is ominously round-faced like an avatar of Harry himself. He is a horrific dwarf, a goblin child, not quite human. If he is magically Lime's imp, then through him Harry attempts to lay the blame for his own murder of the porter on his best friend, Holly. The metaphysics of betrayal.

Lime: "How many dots, old man, could you afford?"

Cultural Center: Holly is kidnapped by a taxi driver. Is it one of Lime's thugs? "Are you going to kill me?" he shrieks. Comically, he is dumped out before the British

Cultural Center where Mr. Crabbit has arranged for him to lecture on the "crisis of faith" in the modern novel. (Holly: "What's that?") Following his lecture, during which he is asked, "Where do you put Mr. James Joyce?", Martins is pursued by true murderers. He flees up a spiraling staircase, then down crumbling flights of concrete stairs. Stairs are everywhere in *The Third Man*, as if to provide access from one logic or metaphysic to another. At one level, Harry is a dear friend, at another a brutal criminal, at another a possessed child intent upon your death.

Police Headquarters: Holly learns the truth about Lime's penicillin racketeering.

Cabaret Bar: Martins drinks off his despair. Girls with pointy breasts dance before him. He doesn't notice. He takes no interest

in pointy breasts. He buys two huge bunches of chrysanthemums from an old woman. Where do these chrysanthemums grow in frosty Vienna? Are these Eliot's flowers blossoming out of the dead land?

Martins: "Mind if I use that line in my next novel?"

Anna's Room: The poignancy of the truth: Appropriate and available though Martins may be, Anna cannot love him. She prefers the memory of Harry to the reality of Holly. The full weight of Hollywood romantic conventions requires a coming-together of Anna and Holly. But Holly can never be anything more for her than Harry's slightly effeminate shadow. She is all worthiness loving the face of the utterly unworthy.

Holly stands at Anna's window hoping to see Lime. "He could be

anybody." Holly doesn't see Harry, but he does see my father.

Certain though I am that it is he, I say nothing to my father. I do not insist on the obvious. I do not wish to hurt him with the obvious. I let the obvious pass. Let him claim what he likes. Let him tell me that he is the severe Colonel Calloway. Let him tell me that he is the glamorous Lime. I will nod and smile. I see all I need to see. I only wish that I could walk around that dark, dying Austrian corner with him, my arm around his shoulder. Just for the company.

Anna: "A person doesn't change because we find out more."

Anna's Street: Harry's first appearance. Holly sees his shoes in a darkened doorway. He takes them for the shoes of a police "tail." He shouts. A woman, awakened by the noise, turns on a second-story light. A slashing diagonal light illuminates Harry's smirking face. Carol Reed catches the flavor of the actual. Streets at night. Lime's shoes—hard, black, and shiny. The surprise for the viewer is as fully emotional as we must imagine it is for Holly. Lime, in his all-black garb, mocks the idea of villainhood. He is cherubic and baby-faced. Is it not little Hansl?

One must wonder, however, what Harry's facial expressions mean. As always, Welles's portrayal borders on the excessive, the hambone high school thespian. He looks surprised, quizzical, embarrassed, whimsical, pouty, sinister, menacing, and naughty in quick succession. Tiny, involuntary waves of emotion seem to ripple across his face.

As Martins approaches Harry, a truck comes between them, and when it has passed, Harry is gone. The echoing sound of Harry's fleeing shoes knocking on the Austrian cobblestones is the very sound of lonely despair. He sprints around the same corner at which Holly had earlier seen my father. And vanishes.

The Great Ferris Wheel: Vienna may be wrecked, but the Great Wheel is still functioning. Holly and Harry meet at it. They rise in one of its roomy cars high over the Prater. It also rises over Europe at mid-century. We are given a hawk's-eye view of the tragic scene.

The attractive and repulsive aspects of Harry's character lock in fierce antagonism. He is at once extravagant and tawdry, lighthearted and lethal. He is, in short, an American. His almost plausible logic: "Would you really feel any pity if one of those dots stopped moving forever? If I offered you £20,000 for every dot that stops, would you really, old man, tell me to keep my money—or would you calculate how many dots you could afford to spare?"

(It is amazing to think of a time when one could "look out" on a world that stretched forth as panorama and veritable landscape. I suppose if Holly and Harry had had a TV in their Ferris wheel car, they could have looked out over America at end-century as well. Lime's depraved idea that people are just "dots" would then be nothing more than the bare fact of the matter. "Death? Don't be melodramatic, Holly. I'm not hurting anyone. Pixelated things don't feel pain. I'm just changing the channel, old man.")

Anna's Dresser Drawer: Lime is not the film's only dehumanizing force. When Colonel Calloway confiscates Anna's love letters from Harry, they are removed back to the station in one of Anna's dresser drawers. (Did they forget to bring a box? a paper bag?) But a close-up of the drawer at the station reveals that there are more than letters here. There is an unfinished embroidery, some small intimate boxes, sachets, and silky kerchiefs. This was all to be taken "downstairs" and "photographed." In the laboratory. Anna, too, is a "dot" for the police. There are no humans left in Vienna, only objects to be manipulated and calculated.

Sergeant Paine: "It's all right, Miss, we're like doctors."

The Trap: The film nears its conclusion. Holly waits in a café for Lime. He is conscious bait. He is betraying Harry. An exotic, perverse balloon seller approaches Calloway and Paine where they wait in darkened ambush. "Bahloon, mein herr?" The film becomes surreal. Who would imagine selling balloons in the midnight dark of a menacing side street? He wears a stagy beard. Is it the cunning Welles/Lime in disguise? Or is this a goofy role Reed found to humiliate my soldierly father?

Suddenly the music thunders in full theme: Harry Lime makes his matchless entry, appearing in silhouette on top of the rubble that was a building, smoking a cigarette, coolly surveying the scene. He is king of the mountain. He is the last man standing. He is one ego aperch a ruined world. But it is the last moment of his grandeur. When he enters the café (gullibly, implausibly, fatally), there are instantaneous whistles and shouts. Dogs bark and sirens shrill. There is a sense of total mobilization. The entire police machinery of Vienna is unleashed on Harry. Ironically, the soldiers wear the helmets worn by the soldiers of the Third Reich. The scene has the appearance, so familiar from other movies of the period, of the SS in pursuit of a victim. Harry escapes, a frightened animal. Apparently, in this world, Nazis of one stripe pursue Nazis of another stripe. The trick is to persuade that there are differences between these "interests" or "zones."

Paine: "Sounds anti-British, Sir."

The Sewers: Suddenly we are tiny creatures, evil children, splashing in the bowels of this city. A great smell trickles here, cascades there. We are lost in a bewildering place: Harry Lime's home. He has escaped to his refuge in the sewers of Vienna. This foulness runs straight to the Blue Danube.

The cinematic effect is thrilling, bewildering. We are lost in this smelly labyrinth. Life cannot possibly live here. The background zither music is silent. There is only

the rush of the sewer water and the desperate, lonely echo of Lime's running footsteps. I recognize it as the sound of the inside of my brain.

Lime comes to an open amphitheater, a central area where many smaller streams meet. He doesn't know which way to run. Voices, each seeming to speak a different language, burst from each tunnel. The languages swirl about him like ghosts. He can't run, but he runs.

Finally, Lime is shot during an exchange of fire with Calloway. He drags himself up one last flight of stairs, Martins just behind him, prepared to be Lime's executioner. But Lime has not yet accepted his death. He pulls himself up the metal stairs to a grill on the other side of which is the world. His fingers thrust through the grill. Abruptly, Reed moves the perspective to the street. We are looking at Harry's fingers emerging through the grill, cut off from the rest of his body. A dry wind rushes indifferently, as if these fingers really emerged from the floor of a desolate canyon. They wriggle hopelessly, pale worms. Grim cheese squeezed through a cloth. This is the truth, behind the world's daylit reality; its "business" is this despair. These detached fingers endowed with an awful will.

"That's it!"
"What?"
"That's it!"
"That's what?"
"Me!"
"You?"
"Me!"
"Those fingers?"
"Those fingers are my fingers! Orson Welles filmed the scene in the sewer weeks before and had returned to Italy, where he was working on

Othello. Mr. Reed needed fingers and I had some.

"Son, I played Harry Lime's fingers in *The Third Man*. There's something to tell your punk friends."

Should I have been happy for my father's brilliant past? Should I have applauded? Said, "Bravo, old man, kudos!'"? Or should I have been appalled that these worm-like objects were his? I stared at him, his smiling, pleased face alternating in my immature mind with the image of his detached wriggling fingers.

One way or the other, that was that. We'd had our mythic evening. It was over with the startling and uncomfortable suddenness of emerging from the magic of a darkened theater into the afternoon sun or, worse yet, a suburban shopping mall. We'd shared. We'd talked. I'd discovered things about my father. But Anna's words kept returning to me: "A person doesn't change because you find out more." Too bad.

Unpredictably, my sisters had emerged from their emblematic poses and were now chattering on the couch with us. They didn't like the movie. It was boring. Why did we always have to watch shows with guns in them? More amazing yet, the general whirl of words and feelings was directing us toward the car, the '59 Dodge Sierra station wagon that sank into the street's tar like a dinosaur into the La Brea. We were going to go "for a ride." It was to be a "family outing." Then you should have heard the din! Chaotic babble. Harry Lime had it good in

---

Glitter

Another fuckwit drops into the dustbin
of history, just as we're finishing our coffee.
Some of us are meant to burn out, is that
right? Like roman candles, across the night sky.

I want to go up like a tree, not a rocket,
I'd like to get drunk disgracefully
with a favorite niece, and grow old
among an amplitude of footnotes.

Pour another Pernod, Famous Poet, and
tell me again about the doomstruck literati,
those dropouts immortalized in ink—your
thirst, your secret greed: your mausoleum.

—John Tranter

those sewers. The tide of family feeling pushed us toward the street. When the car ignited, there was so much enthusiasm that we seemed to be boiling. We were going to blast off, all eight cylinders roaring. The instrument panel lights gave off a phosphorescent green glow in the darkness.

Then Janey said, "What about Mom?"

"Where's Mom?"

"Where has she been all these years?"

"She never does anything with us."

"Let's wait for her."

"Hey, here she comes!"

Indeed it was Mom, hopping across the lawn, laughing, catching up. Finally, it appeared that we were a happy family. What was there to dread in this world? She got in the backseat with my sisters. I could hear them popping like popcorn. But there was also the curious scent that invariably indicated that a few kernels were scorching at the bottom of the pan. I looked back.

In the nervous dark of our family station wagon's backseat I could see the telltale glow of my mother's hair. It was on fire. She had it up in a sort of fetching beehive of embers. It was a torch. It was roaring. But no one seemed to notice but me. Little wisps of charred film floated in the air.

"Roll down your window a little, Butch, it's getting hot in here."

I did as I was told but then looked quickly back again. They were laughing and talking rapidly. They might have been college roommates. But already the torch of my mother's hair had been passed. Janey's brown hair flamed. Winny's blonde hair smoldered. I turned forward.

"Dad . . ."

"What?"

"There's something wrong."

"Like what?" He accelerated. The bleary ooze of tire emerged from the smeary ooze of road. The speedometer struggled forward. We snapped outward. I was pushed back against the seat. We were blasting off for Mars. (Would Holly the Martian meet us there?) I turned again, hoping against hope that I'd been seeing things. I was greeted by three smiles and a solid hedge of flaming brow.

"What are you lookin' at?" they cried together, socking each other in the arm at the hilarious coincidence.

I looked forward. The little toy homes flew by on each side, illuminated by their ridiculously frail porch lights. If someone somewhere, some superior force, were centrifuging our suburb, what liquid would trickle from us?

"Well?" my father asked. "What is it?"

"Nothin'."

Early Poem

"How's everything in Sunny Vale?"
    —Bill Lluoma

My dad would always come home
from his job at the IG Farben (Reichold
Chemicals really) & ask, "How's
every thing in Sunny Vale?" some-

times it would become "Happy Dale"
but i think it was always some private
joke, some strange form of irony—like
he wasn't really expecting anything

to be either Sunny or Happy. I don't
think my mother ever 'got it.' I like
to think that i did. But i was 8. What
was there 'to get' anyway? It was after

the donut shop but before the lawn
business. & by the time he was
working for DRAVO he had given
it up entirely, for more realistic

utterances like, "I was in meetings
all day so I couldn't get any work
done." & i like to think that i'm older
now than he was then, but i know

that's not true, even if i don't do the math.
But i will be someday. That's how it goes
you know. You get older & there's nothing
left of you but the empty shell of a joke.

—Douglas Rothschild

Continued from page 12
is very much a Gannett project. Al Neuharth, the charismatic founder of *USA Today* and the company's public face through the Eighties (today he writes a weekly column for the paper and serves as "Founder" of the Freedom Forum, a journalism think tank once known as the Gannett Foundation), may have been the first prominent newspaperman in the nation to identify cynicism and elitism as the industry's two greatest problems. In his heyday he routinely denounced the newspaper elites "east of the Hudson and east of the Potomac," those purveyors of "intellectual snobbery," "pompousness," and "arrogance" who "think their mission is to indict and convict, rather than inform and educate." But *USA Today* was to be the home of something new, a "Journalism of Hope," in Neuharth's famous phrase, an embodiment of the new middlebrow's refusal to judge: "It doesn't dictate. We don't force unwanted objects down unwilling throats." Generally speaking, Gannett newspapers don't startle, shock, or use long words and difficult concepts. They offer consumers a pleasant product that is remarkably consistent from place to place and that emphasizes reader interaction and "good news."

Critical stories about Gannett are fairly rare; when they do happen to appear, they seem always to revert to the most simplistic of denunciations. The company's literary products are dismissed as lowest-common-denominator stuff; its executives are hooted for their boorish tastes and faintly creepy corporate conformity. But to read Gannett in such a reflexively contemptuous way is to dismiss its very real and very significant theoretical contributions to American culture. Whatever else one might say about it, *USA Today* is arguably the nation's most carefully edited and highly polished newspaper; the way it looks and reads is the result of years of refinement and planning. Certain of its executives may be louts, but from the invention of coverage-by-demographic to color in the masthead to the pseudo-interactive style, *USA Today* has charted the course that almost every paper in the country is presently following. And, of course, Gannett has had a hand in developing the theoretical side of the business as well. The Freedom Forum, staffed by a number of former Gannett executives, sponsors panel discussions featuring thinkers like Rosen and publishes the *Media Studies Journal*, in

Doing Good, Looking Marvelous

Kevin Mattson

In case you haven't heard, Big Government has been safely consigned to the dustbin of history and "the Era of Big Citizenship," as President Clinton announced just on the heels of gutting our social safety net, has dawned. Yes, unlike other nations peopled with diminutive, stunted citizens who continually whine for things like universal health coverage and a functioning infrastructure, our great nation has cast its lot with that most inexhaustible of American resources: native self-reliance. In other words, we're letting the market take care of those who can't take care of themselves. And where the market doesn't avail—that is, in the case of those derelicts who just can't seem to get with the new regime—we've got legions of enthusiastic do-gooders eager to help out. True, our cities have been desolated by redlining, deindustrialization, and suburban sprawl. But we've got the kids. The nice affluent kids, the ones who *care*. They'll paint the walls, repair the roads, tutor the disadvantaged, and clean up the pollution—and they'll do it all for free.

To silence any doubts about America's new civic spirit, in April 1997 Clinton staged the President's Summit on America's Future, a three-day extravaganza of concerts, cheerleading and public-service voluntarism. The basic idea was to evangelize the "MTV generation" in terms it could understand. Rapper LL Cool J kicked off the celebration at Philadelphia's Marcus Foster Stadium, stoking the audience with a nice speech on family values and the importance of volunteering, followed by an evening of stirring oratory and performance from Oprah Winfrey, John Travolta, Michael Bolton, and Brooke Shields. Former Presidents Carter and Bush were on hand to remind us that the stars are not the only ones whose hands steer the great ship of civil society, and Clinton himself, unctuous and televisual as ever, delivered the gooey keynote homily. If at times the proceedings seemed less than dignified for former leaders of the Free World ("We got all the presidents back there waiting to come out here, baby!" bellowed the emcee), well, that's just part of getting through to the kids.

After the hip-hop, the celebrity cameos, and the presidential palaver, it was time to get busy, as the summit's organizers invited a mob of virtuous citizens to descend on Germantown Avenue, one of Philadelphia's poorest neighbor-hoods, for a grand spectacle of stage-managed civic virtue. Along with their celebrity leaders, volunteers painted over graffiti, cleaned up lots, and fixed up parks and playgrounds. The press swarmed over the place, camera lenses and boom microphones jostling to record fleeting moments of caring. The next day the papers carried images of President Bush wiping paint off the face of a young volunteer, Colin Powell cleaning up a vacant lot, and President Clinton leaning on crutches while attempting to paint a wall.

Germantown Avenue locals mostly watched dumbfounded. Many had not been invited to participate, and the invasion of volunteers left them slightly suspicious, wondering when the graffiti would appear again. One neighborhood woman complained that volunteers had painted over store signs by accident. Others gathered at a "People's Summit" to denounce the President's Summit as a cheap photo-op and a boondoggle. For the most part, an unbridgeable gap remained between the do-gooders and the do-goodees. Neighborhood residents "were saying they would clean up the park

which prominent journalists wax ponderous (and apparently unedited) about their weighty responsibilities.

While Gannettoids have not been prominent in the fourth estate's recent circus of contrition, they have joined quite naturally in the chorus of accusation. Each successive disaster to befall the Washington press corps—chased from the field by *Brill's Content* or James Fallows, humiliated by Stephen Glass, routed convincingly in yet another of those poll-driven popularity contests—is a little victory for Gannett, whose once-derided stand against "cynicism" and "elitism" now seems to be vindicated by every new whipping administered to the more respectable news institutions. *USA Today*, in fact, has even begun to take the lead in denouncing the now vulnerable "media elite," deriding the people columnist Samuel Freedman inventively labels "brainiacs," lambasting what Neuharth calls the "would-be Woodwards and Bernsteins (who) came off college campuses," and who have now so shamed their profession through their ignoble desire "to get rich and famous."

Such sanctimoniousness is perhaps the ideal introduction to the painless series of contradictions that make up Gannett's trademark middlebrow sensibility. In fact, according to just about everyone who has ever written about the company, Gannett's curious journalistic style seems to have been consciously invented to permit an extraordinary level of profitability. Realizing early on that owning the franchise in a one-newspaper town can be remarkably lucrative, the company has, since its beginnings, bought or created monopolies across the country. Since the "journalism of hope" often requires little more than press-release rewriting and virtually mandates favorable coverage of local businesses, it can be done both cheaply and with an eye to cultivating advertisers. Critical observers have accused Gannett of slashing both news content and newsgathering staff; of constantly shuffling its editors about the country; of deleting competitors and soaking local advertisers.* The

---

* In February, 1998, Gannett paid the owners of *The Nashville Banner*, an afternoon paper competing with its *Nashville Tennessean*, a reported $65 million simply to close their paper down. Prior to this, advertising space in both papers had been sold jointly, according to a joint operating agreement and based on the two papers' combined circulation. Now one of the papers is no more, but, according to Henry Walker of *The Nashville Scene*, ad prices have still not been lowered.

company is also dogged by strange profit-legends: Veteran journalist Richard McCord relates both the improbable but persistent rumor of the armored cars believed to haul each small-town paper's take off to Gannett HQ and of the company's "dobermans" (ferocious publishing executives) who can be dispatched across the country to put troublesome competitors out of business. Neuharth himself refers to the company as "a nonstop money machine" and approvingly quotes Wall Street figures who call Gannett "virtually an unregulated monopoly" and who note that its "management lives, breathes, and sleeps profits and would trade profits over Pulitzer Prizes any day." Observers of the company marvel at its sumptuous offices and the money-burning antics of Neuharth, who boasts of his "first-class tastes" in his memoirs. And while family-owned newspapers are lucky to make a 10 percent profit in a good year, Gannett routinely squeezes close to 30 percent out of its properties.

The primary casualties of Gannett's corporate culture war are the cities in which the company does business. McCord makes this point thoroughly and repeatedly in his 1996 book *The Chain Gang*, recalling town after town where Gannett's intervention has resulted in relentless downdumbing and the silencing of independent editorial voices. Another consistent victim of Gannett's strategy is organized labor, whose wage scales can impede the astronomical profits that the company demands. "Gannett is among the most antiunion companies that we deal with," says Linda Foley, president of the Newspaper Guild. "They just do not believe that their employees should have collective bargaining rights." One can detect traces of this attitude in *The Making of McPaper*, a panegyric of *USA Today*'s early days by its former editor-in-chief Peter Prichard, who consistently describes union workers as troublemaking thugs bent on keeping "The Nation's Newspaper" from reaching its adoring public. One can see it more clearly in the company's policy of excluding employees "covered by a collective bargaining agreement" (as its annual report puts it) from participation in 401(k) plans and its elevation to a board position of Drew Lewis, who famously busted the air traffic controllers' union while

if they had adequate support," one volunteer explained, "[but] I kind of doubt they would."

In effect, the President's Summit was less about helping the poor revitalize their neighborhoods than about letting the rest of us off the hook for not really giving a hang about Germantown Avenue. Not surprisingly, there has been no apparent follow-up to the torrent of good intentions the summit intended to unleash. Colin Powell, for example, allowing himself to be carried away by the spirit of the moment, suggested that civic organizations (such as his own, called America's Promise) ought to guilt-trip corporations into bankrolling their projects. He seems to have accomplished little more than spooking potential donors, who, according to *Business Week*, regard the Clintonite civic spirit as backdoor socialism. "It could cost billions each year," whined Susan Eckerly of the National Federation of Independent Businesses. A scheme Powell cooked up to raise $10 million from corporations for an advertising campaign on behalf of Big Brothers/Big Sisters of America has raised "practically nothing," according to a report in *The New Republic*.

As federal and state governments increasingly shunt social services to nonprofit and community-based organizations, these groups have come into stiffer competition for foundation funding. Foundations have increased their contributions to human services-oriented programs by 6 percent since 1996—hardly enough to respond to federal spending cuts—even as their endowments swelled with riches from the stock market. Meanwhile, they seem to be as mesmerized as the Democratic Leadership Committee by the prodigal wisdom of the Invisible Hand. Foundation leaders have begun to worry that their subventions and ministrations are a mite too paternalistic—that they, too, may be breeding dependency among the needy. "Most [foundation leaders] choose to limit their funding to short periods in an effort to press grantees to become increasingly self-sufficient," J. Gregory Dees reported earlier this year in the *Harvard Business Review*.

At the same time, corporate contributions to charity have declined radically. In 1986 corporate gifts accounted for 2.3 percent of pre-tax income; by 1996 that figure had dropped to 1.3 percent. In June 1988 the *Chronicle of Philanthropy* reported that corporate contributions rose slightly in 1997 but still accounted for "just 1.1 percent of pre-tax income." More and more corporate leaders are coming around to the view expressed by "Chainsaw Al" Dunlap, ex-CEO of Sunbeam and a notorious union-buster, that corporate philanthropy is an unfair "confiscation" of shareholders' money. "Even in good years, companies are increasing their giving less than the increase in profits," the *Harvard Business Review* reported in 1994. "CEOs are no longer willing to serve as the champion of the giving function." Bill Gates summed up the new mentality of corporate largesse in an interview with *Forbes*: "I feel I can have a positive effect on society by empowering people through our products."

But if traditional corporate philanthropy is drying to a trickle, you wouldn't know it. Everywhere you turn, on television or in newspapers and magazines, on billboards and radio spots, corporate leaders present themselves as empowerers, in accordance with the new Clintonite civic spirit, facilitating the flow of charity dollars through the miraculous workings of the free market. More and more, corporate philanthropy takes the form of what's known as "cause-related marketing," a technique whereby companies advertise their products or services and promote some charity with warm PR appeal. Buy our products, they tell us, and save the world. Typical of these campaigns is "Charge for Hunger," run by American Express, a pioneer of cause-related marketing. Every time a customer makes a purchase with an Amex card, the company donates a small fraction of the charge to Share Our Strength, a nonprofit hunger-relief program. Between

serving as Ronald Reagan's secretary of transportation. And it came into particularly sharp focus in Detroit after Gannett acquired *The Detroit News*.

But the point here isn't just that Gannett practices an unpleasant form of profit-seeking; its remarkably consistent behavior along those lines has been thoroughly documented elsewhere over the years, most recently and most comprehensively by McCord. More remarkable is its melding of populism and predation, the seamless connection the company has forged between its rapacity and its Up With People exterior. It is a uniquely American hybrid of opposites, combining a self-effacing, all-inclusive, anti-elitist editorial style with a shamelessly self-aggrandizing corporate culture and the no-nonsense kicking of worker ass. Gannett has invented a postmodern middlebrow all its own, an elaborate strategy for producing newspapers of a standard quality and profitability, a theory of mediocrity that simulates localness and community concern while striving to offend no one.

The deep thinkers of public journalism are strangely reticent about Gannett (an exception is Cappella and Jamieson, who regard Neuharth's "journalism of hope" as a promising idea), and episodes like the Detroit newspaper strike are one reason why. But perhaps there is a larger reason as well. Gannett, in its typically ham-handed way, has made the convergence between journalistic populism and market forces far, far too obvious. The conglomerate's practices might present the thinkers with a trickier question: Why are foundation millions required to propose an operation that the most ruthlessly profit-minded managers have found quite useful all on their own?

USA Today, Gannett's most visible product, is explicitly aimed at an audience of transient businessmen, the reading material of choice as one jets from sales meeting to sales meeting. But in a mix-up that speaks volumes about American culture of the Eighties and Nineties, it has successfully cast itself as nothing less than the People's Newspaper, the folksy small-town read for a folksy small-town nation. From its colorful page-one polls to its frequent editorial use of the imperial "we," populist pretensions are an essential element of the publication's style. Prichard's book (published not in New York but in good ol' Kansas City) begins with the story of how Neuharth decided on the paper's first day of publication to forgo a complicated story about an assassination in Lebanon and emphasize instead the death of Grace Kelly, the original "people's princess," thereby demonstrating, in Prichard's words, that *"USA Today* would be edited . . . not for the nation's editors, but for the nation's readers." Charles Kuralt, volksgeist shaman of the official media, provided further populist credentials in the book's foreword by describing a Norman Rockwell landscape of honest Western towns dotted with omnipresent *USA Today* vending machines, each one bearing a "four-section, four-color gift from Al Neuharth." So you don't miss the point, Kuralt runs through a list of picturesque locales where he has purchased the paper ("the Holiday Inn in Klamath Falls," "the 7-11 store in Great Bridge, Virginia," "the last bus stop before the road runs out at Homestead Valley, California") and even brings in Alf Landon for a cameo.

But Neuharth himself takes the prize for populist posturing. Virtually every account of his life and deeds dwells on his Midwestern background, his impoverished boyhood in South Dakota, his early efforts at a sports paper in that state, and the way his humble origins reflected those of his employer (in its early days Gannett had been an exclusively small-town chain). In his bizarre 1989 memoir, *Confessions of an S.O.B.*, Neuharth again and again attacks the nation's leading papers for their cynicism and negativity, portraying their coverage of events in foreign countries, their strongly held opinions, and their anxious clamoring after Pulitzer Prizes as loathsome badges of class hauteur. *The New York Times*, for example, is said to have suffered from "intellectual snobbery" and *The Washington Post* to exude an "aura of arrogance." Neuharth himself, meanwhile, "declared war on the good old boys in our business," "said 'no' to the status quo," and wins the plaudits of none other than Carter confidant Bert Lance, who is trotted out to enthuse, "This here Gannett is an all-American company, an all-American company." *USA Today*'s account of Neuharth's retirement described him as a "nemesis of the newspaper elite."

Neuharth's populist tendencies took on an almost demented earnestness in 1987, when he set out on an

1993 and 1997, Charge for Hunger generated roughly $4 million per year—much of which is consumed by advertising and administration costs. Cause-related marketing is the fastest growing form of corporate philanthropy. And it gives perfect expression to America's new civic spirit. We don't even need to leave home or venture beyond the mall to do good acts. We certainly don't need to be taxed. We can be humanitarians simply by performing the most sacred rite of American citizenship in the late twentieth century: shopping.

But even for those who *want* to leave the mall or the couch, the very idea of public service has been transformed by the market into an apolitical, if endearing, lifestyle choice. The one-shot, quick-fix version of service—descending on Germantown Avenue, for example—illustrates just how superficial service has become. Even true believers in the "authenticity" of service are often shockingly naive about the essentially political nature of problems they attempt to tackle. Riffing on the bogus Generation X rhetoric of hard-bitten realism, many young leaders take pains to distance their projects from the fractious protest politics of the Sixties. Too busy "getting things done" (the new slogan for AmeriCorps, President Clinton's public service initiative), the new volunteers don't have time to get mired in political debates—or politics of any sort, for that matter. Paul Loeb, author of *Generation at the Crossroads*, observed this new attitude in an interview with a leader of the Campus Opportunity Outreach League (COOL), a leading youth service organization formed in the mid-Eighties. "[She] stressed COOL's authentic commitment, as opposed to the radical posturing that she associated . . . with her 1960s predecessors," Loeb wrote. " 'We have Macintoshes and modems.' Then she added, 'We live our beliefs. If we say something, we back it up. If we talk about housing, we get involved in housing.' " Service, then, becomes less a moral or political commitment than simply a more "authentic" lifestyle. Once drained of politics and conflict, it becomes a game anyone can play.

Now there's even an organization dedicated to connecting service with celebrity-worship. It's called Do Something, and in the last few years it's become a darling of traditional foundations such as the Pew Charitable Trust as well as corporate sponsors such as MTV and Blockbuster Video. The group's moniker—modeled no doubt on the famous Nike slogan and ringing with lunk-headed pragmatism—aptly conveys its compulsive directionlessness. One of Do Something's central missions is what it calls "messaging"—"creating a culture of cool around community participation." Judging by the organization's publicity organ, BUILD magazine, messaging is mainly a matter of connecting good turns with the names and faces of pop icons, including Do Something's founder, Andrew Shue, star of TV's Melrose Place.

The first thing you notice about BUILD, which is sent out for free to thousands of readers, is its fawning celebrity-worship. The likes of Shaquille O'Neal, Queen Latifah, and LL Cool J typically grace the cover. The second thing you notice is the advertising: Pepsi, Blockbuster, Polo Jeans. The third thing you notice is how the celebrity-worship and advertising work together. BUILD's first issue featured a panegyric to the bottomless generosity of Shaquille O'Neal on page twelve. On page eleven, O'Neal's beaming visage shilled for Pepsi-Cola.

Celebrities, ads, journalism indistinguishable from ads. Not unheard of in contemporary journalism, you say? That's exactly the point. One ad for Visa offered a rather apt summary of Do Something's essential pointlessness: A young woman needs quick cash to attend her friend's wedding. The hipster slogan written in script across the top of the page reads: "Always a Bridesmaid, Never a Bride (It's cool, I'm not a big fan of commitment.)" Welcome, readers, to the real reason for BUILD.

Here's the new ethic of service, as elaborated in the Shaquille O'Neal profile. The Lakers star, it seems, likes to spend the odd afternoon cruising "depressed neighborhoods." Here he'll "pick out a rundown house where kids live and walk in with a shiny new TV set bobbing along on a

elaborate national tour called "BusCapade." Ostensibly inspired by his conviction that the "national media" had "too much of an East Coast perspective," Neuharth began his tour at the most middling place in the land (a town in Missouri that was then the demographic center of the country), declaring in the first words of his first column that "People hereabouts are proud of being more middlemost than most of us. . . ." In the months of BusCapading that followed, he narrated for USA Today readers his Kuraltian wanderings amongst the people—chin-chinning with lots of just-folks, holding plenty of "town meetings," and conducting polls wherever he went—and led readers toward that iridescent goal of public journalists everywhere: "Understanding. Of each other. All across the USA." What this meant in practice was that Neuharth wrote an installment of his column, "Plain Talk," from every state, celebrating each one successively in ever-more passionate terms. Most of his BusCapade dispatches were organized around some state motto or song or other almanac-level fact whose profundity Neuharth would consider in his usual truncated style. Maryland, for example, struck him as being the place where the national anthem had been composed: "Folks in Maryland think that very appropriate. They consider their state a miniature of the nation. 'America in miniature,' says a slogan." Virginia, he wrote, is both "for lovers" and "the Mother of Presidents." In New Jersey, he observed that the "nickname 'The Garden State' applies." Kansans were said to "like it at home on the range. Seldom is heard a discouraging word." Throw in an occasional stray cliché like "Olympic dreams," a softball interview with a governor or two, and some stories about local entrepreneurs and industries on the rebound, and you've just about got it.

Neuharth's BusCapade exploits bring to mind the emptiest variety of American political demagoguery—one thinks of Richard Nixon's foolish promise to visit all fifty states during the 1960 campaign and of Bill Clinton's own 1992 series of "BusCapades." Not only did Neuharth serve as Clinton's "informal bus consultant," according to Business Week, but he was perhaps the only national newspaper columnist to regard Clinton's bus-stunts as expressions of genuine populist feeling, a sentiment which, he insisted in USA

Today, the "media effete don't understand." One might also read BusCapade as a long-delayed answer to "These United States," the famous series of articles run by *The Nation* in the Twenties in which an all-star cast of intellectuals and eggheads flayed each state in turn for being the home of dolts, bigots, boobs, and philistines. (Also as a delayed riposte to Ken Kesey's famous bit of bourgeoisie-annoying on wheels: The music Neuharth chose to blare from his bus's loud-speakers was not loopy, irritating rock but uplifting state songs, one for each state.)

The high point of BusCapade, in both Neuharth's and Prichard's accounting, was the moment in which Neuharth himself, polling and town-halling his way across the country in a valiant battle against media cynicism, received the tidings of entrepreneurial victory. A telegram arrived announcing *USA Today*'s first-ever month of profitability, by coincidence, just as the Bus was Capading through Al's home state of South Dakota. The achievement thus became something of a populist miracle: local boy borne home on clouds of money. One can imagine the scene, depicted in heroic oversize in the National Gallery or something—"Annunciation of Profits in the Heartland" or "Tycoon's Return." That is, one could have imagined it, had Neuharth not announced in his *Confessions* that the whole thing was a set-up, that he had arranged to have the telegram sent to himself. Strangely, the founder of *USA Today* doesn't seem to think this revelation casts any shade on the event. But pity poor Peter Prichard, whose Neuharth-authorized account solemnly gives the magical version of the event, even reproducing the (staged) telegram of glory.

The incident helps to get at the meaning of the new middlebrow typified by Neuharth, Gannett, and the larger theories of public journalism. This is a populism in which "the people" aren't so much the

huge shoulder." And if no parent or legal guardian happens to be there to accept this prized appurtenance of the good life? Well, Shaq then "typically hangs around and watches a couple of shows on the new set with the kids." What a guy! Perhaps not wanting to cross a boundary of journalistic ethics, the writer neglected to mention whether Shaq drops off half-racks of Pepsi as well.

BUILD caught a lot of flak for its puff piece on O'Neal, and since then the editors and designers of the magazine have become a bit more savvy. But not much. The second issue's cover story on Rage Against the Machine, one of America's "alternative" bands, listed front groups of the wacky, Maoist Revolutionary Communist Party to contact for more information. More revealing, however, were the band's thoughts about activism and the role of the stars. "We try to help people empower themselves," the band's guitarist explained. "We tried in different cities where we played to organize around an issue which we knew would matter to people in our audience, which was music censorship. You can preach all day long to kids in suburban Illinois about United Farm Workers or something—but when they can't buy the new Cypress Hill record,

that's something that's much more concrete." Don't deny those kids their records, for who knows what sort of revolutionary fervor they'll whip themselves into. They might even "do something." Extolling the virtues of consumption now is not only service but downright revolutionary activity.

BUILD's third issue didn't get much better. Its cover story detailed rap star and sitcom actress Queen Latifah's efforts to help "young people . . . control their destinies" by inviting them into her company, where they "master" important skills like "marketing and promotion." Once again, doing good is essentially expanding the market.

Shaquille O'Neal may not be a parasite, Rage Against the Machine may not be nincompoops, and Queen Latifah may realize that her gesture is largely meaningless. Who really cares? The real question is, Why the hell are foundations and others throwing money at Do Something when The Neighborhood Works, a magazine making real contributions to public service, is on the ropes; and when other youth-oriented organizations—such as Unplugged, a group dedicated to ridding schools of commercial encroachment—struggle to keep afloat?

The answer may very well come from none other than LL Cool J, the star of the President's Summit on America's Future and the cover boy of BUILD's Spring 1998 issue. The magazine's interviewer makes little sense of LL's ramblings. Sure, LL makes some nice side remarks about taking "care of your fellow human beings" and talks about a camp that he sponsors. But then, in response to a question about injustice, he blurts out: "Injustice—it's all just a test. Pursue your dreams. Looking at most people in the world, most people, what they say they want and what they think about all the time always seem to be two different things. You have people say 'I want a million dollars,' and then they go in the house and smoke cigarettes and watch sitcoms all night. You're not doing nothing about that million dollars." Sounds

hero as they are a symbol, an ideological figurehead for the larger democracy of the market. Neuharth's constant attacks on the "media elite," for example, seem always to come back to questions of business know-how, in particular the idea that snobs are, by definition, poor entrepreneurs. The newspaper "elite never really considered me an insider," Neuharth remarks at one point, just before relating how the publisher of the hated *Washington Post*, arrogant to the core, once lost a bidding war to him by "thinking her insider club membership would protect her interests." Within pages Al bests her again in yet another takeover contest, this time because she has foolishly sent "Ivy League reporters to Iowa to report on the farm economy," and thus misjudges the true worth of *The Des Moines Register*. Similarly, Al explains that he beat out *The New York Times* in another deal simply because that paper's publisher was "elitist to the end."

So closely are populism and the market connected for Neuharth that it hardly seems contradictory when he turns directly, as he so frequently does in his *Confessions*, from celebrating the plain-spoken ways of the heartland to an almost pathological boasting about the perks of power. With a certain pride he recounts his loudest acts of conspicuous consumption, rattling off the once-impressive brand names—the Porsche sunglasses, the Gulfstream IV jet (with shower), the uniforms worn by the crew of said jet, the Cristal champagne, the "beachside chapel" in his yard where he gives thanks, the luxury hotel suites in which he does business. Nor does Neuharth's dedication to The People and the "Journalism of Hope" prevent him from writing his memoirs as a diary of corporate megalomania. Stories are constantly interrupted so Neuharth can give an account of how somebody praised him or how he burned someone. Almost every chapter begins with a quotation about Chairman Al. And through it all, the only overt explanation Neuharth offers for his doings is the down-home logic of "having fun," or, better yet, "having a helluva lot of fun."

But Neuharth's ideas deserve to be taken seriously nevertheless. Along with the public journalism reformers, Neuharth believes that the decline of the American newspaper is a parable of fundamental democratic virtues. Elitism is what is killing newspapers; getting

Incroyable.

in touch with the common people through polls, focus groups, and town-hall meetings is what will save them. But what is "elitism," exactly? For Neuharth, who seems to hear the Vox Populi even when riding in his corporate jet, the term has little to do with its traditional connotations of economic power. Elitism is a sin committed by authors, not by owners. Elitism is nothing less than critical thought, a failure to exercise that middle-class suspension of judgment so celebrated by Alan Wolfe. Tellingly, this is a lesson that Neuharth chooses to put in the mouth of none other than Lee Kuan Yew, the Singapore strongman who has made public gum-chewing a felony: "The more you judge others by your own standards," this beacon of the General Will tells him, "the more you show total disregard for their circumstances."

In Gannett-land the suspension of judgment is called "listening" to readers, refusing to "dictate" to them. It is accomplished through a number of devices allowing journalists to understand the community for which they write. Polls not only appear every day in each section of *USA Today*, but they seem to hold a hallowed place in company lore. Prichard recalls how Neuharth discovered polling back in the Sixties; how he used it to launch a new newspaper in Florida; and, most significantly, how a batch of market research appeared at just the right moment in 1981 and put Neuharth's arguments for launching a new national newspaper over the top. By 1998, the democratic logic of polling is so familiar to readers that one *USA Today* feature—"Ad Track," a series of studies revealing how "key target groups" feel about various TV commercials—actually equates consumer activism with participating in a focus group, with thinking about how you might best be sold running shoes or fruit drinks.

"News 2000" is the name of Gannett's comprehensive program for "tailoring the content" of a newspaper anywhere in the country with the help of polling and focus groups. It is a theoretical program as well, informed by a vision of the news crisis that directly links the company's corporate populism with anti-intellectualism. A primary factor in the long decline of American journalism, one News 2000 document asserts, is that "some newspapers grew increasingly out of touch with their communities."

like the fulminations of a libertarian Republican. But maybe LL's remarks are like the arguments made by the philanthropists of yore about the "undeserving poor." Maybe LL Cool J is saying that only those who want to become celebrities themselves—those who pursue their dreams of a million dollars—deserve the blessings of the culture industry and its humanitarian causes.

Whatever the meaning of LL Cool J's remarks, they make clear just how vapid the recent American celebration of voluntary service and regenerated civic spirit has become. Rock stars as humanitarians. Painting over graffiti as solving the problems of the inner city. The market as social savior. Meanwhile, the public sector is dismantled, and the inner cities sink into nihilism. This isn't to say that the state should or would take care of all our problems without local initiatives on the part of citizens. America has a strong tradition of citizens organizing together to demand social justice. In the hype about voluntarism lurks the shadow of Saul Alinsky—a community organizer who cut his teeth back in Chicago in the Thirties. In contrast to the pseudo-populism of the President's Summit, Alinsky organized citizens for a long process of political education and confrontations with landlords, developers, and other local political powers. Taking back control over their communities required long-term commitment. Alinsky believed that in order to revive American democracy, citizens needed to be involved in solving local problems. But he knew the tougher side of such struggle, a toll of frustration and heartbreak that neither Bill Clinton nor the lowliest grant-writer at Do Something could ever fathom.

A true renewal of America's civic spirit would embrace heroes like Alinsky. It would resist the ideological onslaught against Big Government. It would fight to reinvigorate public works programs and demand basic rights like universal health coverage. Of course, it would have to recapture Alinsky's fighting spirit as well. Where the corporate cheerleaders for our civic renewal today glorify the market, Alinsky spoke truth to those who wielded economic power over regular citizens. Instead of the pseudo-populism of spectacle voluntarism, Alinsky believed in working with citizens to organize for a long-term struggle for power. The Era of Big Citizenship won't address our social problems or enhance our ailing democracy. That much is sure. But whether or not the community organizers and citizen activists of tomorrow can repair this botched mission remains to be seen.

Continued from page 45

Lakewood and Lakeside Pl.   5-30   11:51 AM
Complaint of male subjects fishing and drinking by lake, unfounded.

Parkside

17100 block Forestview   5-19   8:53 PM
Resident advised male white subject took his Schwinn Predator and rode into wooded area; bike found near Devil's Hill, returned to owner.

Memorial Park   5-20   8:25 PM
Complaint of number of juveniles trying to tip over outhouse, park security notified.

Brementowne Villas

Sussex & Oxford   5-8   7:33 AM
Report of large garage sale in area, vehicles parked on wrong side of street, no illegal parkers on officer arrival.

6800 block Windsor   5-8   8:20 PM
Report of campfire in front yard, settled by officer.

Oxford & Sussex   5-23   6:14 PM
Report of solicitors at resident's house, sprayed vehicle with cleaning substance, resident does not want, solicitors have no permit; located and advised to cease until obtain permit.

16300 block Oxford   5-31   1:12 PM
Report of 2 male subjects beating up each other and each other's cars, settled by officer.

Sundale

175th St. & Odell   5-3   2:04 PM
Complaint of juveniles throwing rocks at geese near pond, GOA [gone on arrival].

17300 block Oriole   5-11   7:30 AM
Suspicious male white subject headed toward school, located and shagged from area.

17100 block Oleander   5-14   8:27 PM
3 male subjects roller blading on street, GOA.

Bristol Park

7700 block Bristol Park   5-10   1:24 AM
Complaint of loud music from car radio in garage, located and advised.

7800 block Marquette   5-13   7:10 PM
Sometime between 6:30 am and 5 pm persons unknown took rollaway grass container.

Bristol Parkway   5-13   8:31 PM
Reports of juveniles throwing things on railroad tracks, GOA.

7800 block Joliet Dr.   5-23   10:37 PM
Report of subject ringing doorbell for past 5 minutes, GOA.

7700 block Marquette   5-25   5:50 PM
Report of kids near construction site destroying portable toilet, unable to locate.

Continued on page 106

They became "arrogant." They "operated 'inside-out' with staffers deciding what news and information was needed by their community, often without a good sense of the concerns of the many groups comprising the community." But Gannett has the answer to such tragic errors: Use focus groups, surveys, and "trend watchers" to help newspapers conform more closely to the wishes of the public. Only then, with "two-way communication between residents and readers," can the newspaper in question "empower residents to improve their lives" and "help to establish newspapers as a 'member of the family' in their communities." The 1997 Gannett annual report further defines the qualities of the non-cynical, non-elitist newspaper: "positive stories," "stories that tell how new developments in the community have a positive effect on citizens and profiles that tell how local business owners have overcome obstacles." *

Reading through Gannett's vision of the community- and owner-affirming newspaper, one can't help but think of the sort of writing that it would prohibit. From William Lloyd Garrison to Lincoln Steffens to I.F. Stone, what few transcendent moments American journalism can boast have each arisen from vicious, even violent conflict between an "inside-out" writer and a furiously intolerant "community," usually a "community" made up of precisely those "local business owners" whom Gannett designates as the beneficiaries of its brand of empowerment. One also thinks of public journalist Mark Willes, whose brand of civic service encompasses both dedication to profit and what sounds like a war on critical thought itself. Soon after deciding to tear down the wall between editorial and business in a quest to make the *Los Angeles Times* more profitable, Willes announced that in order to make female readers "feel like the paper's theirs" it needed to come up with stories that were "more emotional, more personal, less analytical." Wherever newspaper moguls talk populism and profits simultaneously, it seems, the practical results take the same form: a sort of middle-class relativism in which tenaciously held ideas are the greatest journalistic error of all.

---

* *The Cincinnati Enquirer*'s fairly ferocious attack on Chiquita (a company whose chairman, significantly, once attempted a hostile takeover of Gannett) would seem an exception to this rule, were it not for the singular abjectness of the apology to Chiquita that the paper ran shortly thereafter.

What must be kept constantly in mind while pondering Gannett's ideal of the hopeful, happy newspaper, though, is that all this democratic talk goes hand in hand with a particularly adamantine species of corporate practice. Needless to say, Gannett's way of doing business is absolutely and utterly non-negotiable, as subject to the public will as the coming and going of cold fronts. (Nor does the company's penchant for "listening" include tolerance for criticism: *The Nashville Scene* reports that a Gannett editor in that city recently tried to prevent critic McCord from speaking at a meeting of Nashville's Society of Professional Journalists.) There is an important distinction, though, between Gannett's market populism and the organic middlebrow of decades past: If we learn anything from the literature surrounding *USA Today* it is that superhuman efforts, both intellectual and physical, were required to put this most inoffensive of newspapers over. We read about the deeds of Neuharth's hand-picked team of "geniuses" charged with inventing this masterpiece of mediocrity, about the tweaking of the prototypes and the response from the focus groups, about Neuharth's dictatorial leadership style, about his close editing of the newspaper's stories, about the people who couldn't take the rigorous pace and gave up. What is described is not merely the launching of a national newspaper, but the heroic forging of a new middlebrow by a man who is simultaneously hard as screws and soft as flan, absolutely determined, with a Calvinist inner fire, to be other-directed.

Pro Patria et Pro Gannett: The Monument

"FREEDOM of the press," goes the old leftist saying, "belongs to those who own one." It is a cynical adage, to be sure, the scoffing negation of Al Neuharth's tendency to refer to even the "biggest media companies" with the possessive pronoun "our." And, as with all the other bits of cynicism so deplored by recent critics of journalism, it can have no place in the aggressively public-minded age into which "our biggest media companies" are leading us.

Stamping out this and any other suggestion that journalism, properly practiced, might be guided by interests other than "ours" is the noble charge taken

Color Me Middle
Doug Henwood

If there's one thing that's certain about us Americans, runs the national myth, it's that we're a democratic bunch. We're almost universally middle class. Oh, sure, there are some smelly vagabonds wandering the streets of our big cities, a few illiterate hillbillies in Tennessee hollers, and Bill Gates, but otherwise, we're all just ordinary normal middle-class folks.

Recently, though, doubts have crept in, as the economy has thinned out the middle class, separating us once again into a nation of rich and poor. Should we be worried? Not according to sociologist Alan Wolfe, who has arrived on the scene just in time to assure us that, as the title of his book puts it, we are *One Nation, After All*. (And get a load of the book's subtitle: *What Americans Really Think About God, Country, Family, Racism, Welfare, Immigration, Homosexuality, Work, The Right, The Left and Each Other*, Viking Press, hardcover, $24.95). Wolfe has studied the middle-class American mind, and—guess what?—he's found it largely free of alienation, status anxiety, and bigotry. His Americans are tolerant (except for when they have to think about those queers), open-hearted (except toward the wrong kind of immigrants), and ceaselessly striving. They also seem to be deeply confused, utterly depoliticized, and convinced of contradictory things that neither they nor Wolfe bother to investigate, let alone resolve.

Maybe the best comment on Wolfe's awful book came from a waitress who asked me what I was reading as she brought me a beer. I showed the cover to her, with its subtitle, "What middle class Americans think about. . . ." She asked if it was any good. No, I answered, it's a boring, mushy, terrible book. "Well," she explained, "that's because we don't think anything interesting."

Wolfe makes his biggest blunder right on the first page. "According to the General Social Survey," he writes, "at no time between 1972 and 1994 did more than 10 percent of the American population classify themselves as *either* lower class or upper class" (yes, emphasis in the original). That means, according to Wolfe's specious reasoning, that the remaining 90 percent would call themselves "middle class." In fact, they wouldn't. When given the choice, a majority of the American population has consistently identified itself as "working class."

But Wolfe does not intend to give them that choice. He is a man on a mission—to probe the "middle-class" mind and then provide his affluent readers 359 pages worth of nice reassurance about themselves. To take the measure of middle-class thought, Wolfe and his "Middle Class Morality Project" first chose eight suburbs in different parts of the country, strangely but intentionally skewing their choices to favor affluent, conservative, religious places (the book begins with a heartwarming homage to each charming burg). From the population of those suburbs Wolfe and Co. then chose a number of individuals (again skewing their sample toward the affluent), questioned them about their thoughts on life, and then "coded" their responses numerically. And since, as everyone knows, America is a suburban nation, the charts, graphs, and banal prose that result become what "we" think.

This curious methodology virtually determines the book's conclusions. It also seems to have determined the book's enthusiastic reception by mainstream publications and politicos, all of them dazzled by the prospect of a hardy consensus thriving all this time out there in suburbia. The source of Wolfe's magic touch seems to be his ability to portray the average American as a reflection of the opinion-making class itself:

up by the Newseum, a museum of journalism recently opened across the street from the glass towers of the Gannett/*USA Today* complex in Arlington, Virginia. This latest Neuharth project was built by the Freedom Forum, of which he is "Founder" and former chairman; some official documents also list Neuharth as the Newseum's "Founder" so there is no mistake, while the executive director of the complex was until recently none other than Neuharth hagiographer Peter Prichard. Promising to transform the great man's deeds into history, his strange ideas into wisdom for the ages, the Newseum is the sort of project that will someday be mandatory for retiring megalomaniacs.

In keeping with Neuharth's peculiarly populist megalomania, the Newseum has banished the elitist devices of the traditional museum, all the formal traces of the patriarchal, the pompous, the pontificating. Its curving, open-ceilinged halls are filled with working video equipment, interpreters for the deaf, and computer stations on which people can try their hands at reporting and editing.

An introductory Newseum filmstrip declares: "We're all reporters, because each of us tells stories." Mastheads from our hometowns help situate us on the "News Globe"; headlines from our dates of birth tell us who we are. The press is your pal, we learn. The press is you. In fact, the press is your memory, your consciousness, your conscience. Screens scattered throughout the history exhibits remind us of those journalistic moments—almost all of them disasters of one sort or another—that are increasingly all we have in common as a nation. Here Walter Cronkite announces the death of JFK; there Frank Reynolds briefly loses his cool while announcing the shooting of Reagan; and over in a corner falls a little hailstorm of emotional news moments from more recent years: an endlessly repeating pitter-pat of "We interrupt this program" and announcements that "Princess Diana [pause] has died"; an exciting hijacking and baby Jessica caught in a well; glimpses of parents realizing that their daughter has exploded with the space shuttle, of the screen going blank as Scuds fall on Israel.

Strangely, almost every one of these episodes ranks, for less ecstatic critics, among American journalism's all-time lows. But at the Newseum there is no sense of shame or even acknowledgment of such criticism. Quite the opposite: Here these poignant moments of reporter-audience closeness are presented as the crowning glories of a centuries-long struggle against tyranny. It's a tendency one notices again and again here. While the Newseum's facade is all open-ended and egalitarian, the handful of serious points it makes are hammered home in a style so Whiggishly presumptuous that one might as well be learning about the advance of empire or the conversion of savages. The "News History Gallery," the museum's serious (and at times impressive) collection of historical artifacts, is as bombastic a tale of Progress and its millionaire heroes as anything invented by the commissars in their heyday. Beginning from the earliest colonial publications, and taking us through the rise of yellow journalism and the twentieth-century tabloids, the gallery deposits us neatly before the *USA Today* exhibit ("The Newspaper is Reinvented"), the story of the media conglomerates, and the endless loop of Jessica, *Challenger*, and [pause] Diana, a fabulous *now* in which the emotional needs of The People are seen to efficiently. Just ahead lies "interactivity," the cultural-democratic New Jerusalem where authorial voice is finally dissolved in the ecstatic communion of journalist and audience. Pulitzer, Hearst, Neuharth, You.

Assuming you are among that vast majority of Americans who regard journalists with contempt, and can therefore see right through such stuff, the Newseum has an even more compelling narrative to offer: The heroic tale of the press as selfless champion of democracy, as an ever-advancing libertarian tide whose flow cannot be impeded and whose every move is a step forward for We the People. "Information is where liberty starts," intones the narrator of the introductory filmstrip, and the theme continues as one follows the glorious march of historical progress. Tyrants try to suppress press; but press suppresses tyrants. The invention of the moving-picture

prosperous, self-satisfied, and a little weary of conflict. Wolfe's "findings" about the middle class—that it shuns divisiveness, values consensus, and is well-meaning in virtually everything it says and does—are flattering in the extreme. The idea of class itself is the primary victim: Class doesn't shape or constrain us, it doesn't determine our values or world views, it doesn't divide us against each other. In the great middle, among the 90 percent, moral issues matter more than political ones, individual interests eclipse collective ones.

For Wolfe's middle, in fact, politics seems to be something of a cuss word. Religion is thought to be marvelous as long as it's not "political"; ditto multicultural education and patriotism, even. Wolfe interprets this attitude as "tolerant," but what he means is "indecisive." Neither religion nor culture seems to make any demands on these Americans. As Wolfe helpfully writes: "Ambivalence—call it confusion if you want to—can be described as the default position for the American middle class; everything else being equal, people simply cannot make up their minds."

Wolfe's middle class just isn't interested in the big questions. Their religion is tepid; their tolerance contentless; and their taste in virtues is decidedly "modest," personal, "writ small." The activating principle seems to be an abiding horror of disagreement. "Virtue, like religion, cannot be equated with politics," Wolfe writes, "for that would lead to division and discord."

It's amazing how much Wolfe's

middle triumphant sounds like the USSR in its heyday, post-Gulag and pre-Gorby. Here's Henri Lefebvre's description of the moral code of *Homo sovieticus* from the early Sixties:

This code can be summed up in a few words: love of work (and work well done, fully productive in the interests of socialist society), love of family, love of the socialist fatherland. A moral code like this holds the essential answer to every human problem, and its principles proclaim that all such problems have been resolved. One virtue it values above all others: being a 'decent' sort of person, in the way that the good husband, the good father, the good workman, the good citizen are 'decent sorts of people . . . .'

Change "socialist" to "American," and you've pretty much got it.

Technically speaking, Wolfe's "Middle Class Morality Project" is a joke; it's hard to imagine this passing review at a scholarly journal. But Wolfe is obviously more interested in ideological celebration than telling the truth. "In a nutshell," Wolfe asserts, "what middle-class Americans find distinctive about America is that it enables them to be middle class. Unlike India or Japan, the very rich and the very poor are smaller classes here, and opportunity enables those with the desire and the capacity to better their lot in life." But even this is wrong. India is poor in absolute terms, but, according to World Bank figures, the country's distribution of income isn't all that different from the United States. And of all the First World countries, the United States has the *most polarized* distribution of income, the *smallest* middle class (measured relative to average incomes), an *average* level of general mobility, and a *terrible* record on upward mobility out of the income basement. Statistically speaking, the U.S. is one of the most class-divided societies on earth.

Class, of course, is the greatest and most divisive bogeyman of all for Wolfe's "middle class." It cannot be discussed, and Wolfe

camera, for example, brings forth this astonishingly counterfactual remark: "The citizens now know they have a powerful ally in the hunt for the truth." But in the hands of the Newseum's curators, obviously concerned to make the point about the goodness of journalists as hard to miss as possible, the story rapidly descends from the enlightening—there is actually an exhibit on W.E.B. Du Bois's magazine *The Crisis*—to a mawkish obsession with the persecution of journalists, as though that alone were enough to establish their essential decency. A rather irrelevant quotation in which Thomas Jefferson mentions both "freedom of the press" and "martyrdom" appears on pamphlets and an outside wall. Scenes of Dan Rather in China are accompanied by the solemn observation that "Reporters have been censored, jailed, sometimes killed for doing their job." One exhibit lingers libidinally over the physical dangers faced by reporters during the Gulf War (presumably as they were shuttled around in those closely chaperoned army pools).

Those who still doubt the democratic commitment of the press can visit "Freedom Park," a collection of weather-proof souvenirs of The Struggle mounted next to a sidewalk outside: One relic each from the fights for women's suffrage, civil rights, and the battles against Nazis and apartheid, and no fewer than three from the war against Communism. None of them have much to do with journalism, of course, but T-shirts depicting the inspiring objects can be purchased in the Newseum store, along with copies of Al Neuharth's memoirs, still clean and full-priced although published nearly eight years ago and readily available in thrift stores nationwide.

When a Fortune 500 company (or its prodigal philanthropic stepchild) takes up public moaning about persecution, one is permitted a little skepticism. And the Newseum's historiography is suspicious stuff indeed, oblivious to vast regions of the American experience even as it goes out of its way to hail the achievements of just about every approved social or political struggle. As told by the News History Gallery, the march of liberty includes feminism and the civil rights movement, the fights against Hitler and communism, dozens of individual battles against racism and sexism, and victory after victory for champions of free speech. It makes no mention—none—of the fight for the eight-hour day and for the right of workers to unionize in the last century, or of the various reforms won by labor in this century, or of which side "our" friendly "media companies" were on in those struggles. And the closer one looks the more apparent this erasure becomes: William Allen White is lauded for opposing the Klan and for supporting free speech, but his Progressivism somehow never comes up. *The Masses* makes it into the museum because it was "banned from the mail for opposing U.S. participation in World War I," but the logic of its opposition is not discussed. The Newspaper Guild, which represents reporters and editors at any number of American newspapers, is mentioned only in a short bio of its founder, Heywood Broun. And "working class" is used almost exclusively as a demographic notation, as in its "relish" for tabloids and affinity for certain Hearst columnists.

The Newseum's consistent evasion of class is part of a more sinister reticence about the seamier side of the trade. The chronic journalistic problem of keeping editorial separate from business, for example, no doubt familiar to veterans of any Gannett paper, is mentioned nowhere. The "Ethics Center," where one may grapple

dutifully skews his study so that it need not be. Still, class hasn't completely faded from the American consciousness. In 1949, Richard Center asked a sample of Americans to place themselves in one of four classes—middle, lower, working, or upper. Just over half—51 percent—identified themselves as working class. In 1996, the General Social Survey (GSS), a near-yearly inventory of what Americans own, think, and feel, found, after decades of highly publicized farewells to the working class, 45 percent still called themselves by that name. A *New York Times* poll that year found that 47 percent identified themselves as working class, 40 percent as middle class, 8 percent as lower class, and 3 percent as upper class. Two ABC polls that year asking people to place themselves in either of two classes found 55 percent said working class, while 44 percent said middle class.

In other words, unless you confront the existence of the working class, you aren't talking about middle America. But the myth of universal affluence persists nonetheless. In their very useful book *The American Perception of Class*, Reeve Vanneman and

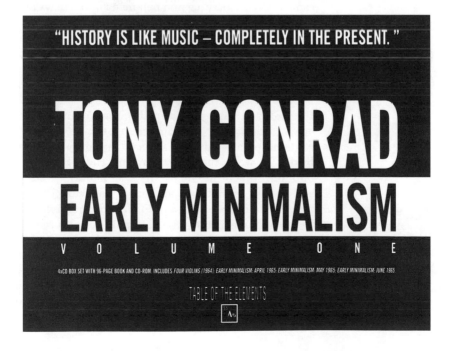

Lynn Weber Cannon show that the tendency to understand the upper reaches of the working class as part of a broad, prosperous, and generally content middle class is itself a reliable class marker, an intellectual habit of the affluent, who like to fancy themselves average people. People of more modest means, on the other hand, tend to divide the world between the upper class and everyone else.

Though the disappearance of class is an old American story, we're in a particularly blind moment these days, with all sorts of silly talk about the democratization of ownership spawned by the bull market. But consider this passage, the most interesting statistic in Wolfe's narcotic book: "In 1939, while America was experiencing a Great Depression right out of Karl Marx's playbook, 25 percent of the American people believed that the interests of employers and employees were opposed, while 56 percent believed they were basically the same. By 1994, when unions and class consciousness were in steep decline, the percentage of those who believed that employers and employees had opposite interests had increased to 45 percent, while those who thought they were the same had decreased to 40 percent." Wolfe brings up the point only to drop it; he's too busy hauling loads of reassurance to and from the land of cul-de-sacs and gated communities. But it gets at the heart of what he is doing and why. If so many people continue to believe our society is structured around conflict, not consensus, we must be close to crisis indeed. Hence the urgency of such bland, comforting, scholarly-sounding niceness: Paradise really *is* ours.

with "the difficult choices faced by journalists every day" (typical dilemma: how to cover a wheelchair-bound president), fails to discuss how one might deal with the misdeeds of a local business that advertises in your paper. Even the exhibit on conglomerates, while acknowledging that the Culture Trust has been criticized, invokes the tired Press vs. Tyranny canard in this remarkable bit of casuistry: "Executives say the size of their corporations helps them stand up to governments that would control news." It's a view of liberty that consistently understands "freedom" as a thing wrung from an inherently repressive state by inherently liberating media corporations: That liberty might have an economic dimension, that the corporations themselves might sometimes be repressive and the state liberating is simply left out, as though contrary to the physical laws of the universe.

But then the goal here is hardly to mount a complex analysis of society. Like other Washington edifices, the Newseum is an exercise in patriotic instruction, an easily absorbed lesson in Why We're So Darn Good. The point isn't to condemn the state on a specific list of charges, but to drive home the underlying principle of recent press theory: We, too, are the state. You may despise us, and we may even be slipping into obsolescence, but the checking and balancing of the news media are as critical to the preserving of nice moderate moderation as are all those other purveyors of museums—from the U.S. Postal Service to the Supreme Court—on the other side of the Potomac.

Other troubled industries have also confronted their persecutors by symbolically comparing themselves to the state (as bankers did in the late Twenties), but one exhibit at the Newseum manages to top them all in its desperate bid for gravitas. On a gray concrete bridge between the Newseum and the USA Today building stands the "Journalists Memorial," a steel-and-glass monument to newspapermen, cameramen, and TV announcers killed in the line of duty. Like the Vietnam Memorial on the National Mall, its centerpiece is a bogglingly comprehensive tally of inscribed names, the sheer number of dead journalists impressing visitors with the magnitude of the fourth estate's sacrifices. Otherwise, though, it is the Vietnam Memorial's opposite: Colorful and fully above-ground rather than pitch-black and sunken, it immediately calls to mind the curiously durable inverse relationship, in public opinion, between the military and the press since the publication of the Pentagon Papers—or since the moment cynical newspaperman David Janssen dared to question John Wayne's war in *The Green Berets*.

Today, of course, the tables are turned: As Al Neuharth pointed out in a recent column, journalists are hated now while soldiers— always imagined these days as a cross between Schwarzeneggerian powerboys and victimized subalterns, kicking ass with a tear in their eye—are revered. Maybe Al came up with the idea for the Journalists Memorial (it certainly bears the earmarks of a Neuharth project) in a poll-inspired epiphany, after poring one long, grim night over the figures that revealed how right-thinking Americans now hold not the long-suffering Nam vet but the reviled newsman responsible for losing that fine war—and maybe the idea of building the Cenotaph of the Fallen Scribe just flashed through his mind, like all his other bits of monumental aggrandizement must have done: the plan for the cross-country bus ride, the discovery that he needed to hire his own pollster (in fact the very one who, he recalls in his memoirs, helped "Jack" Kennedy win "crucial primaries"), the stratagem by which astronaut Alan Shepard was persuaded to take a copy of a Gannett newspaper to the moon, or the inspired decision to enclose with each copy of his *Confessions* a campaign-style button bearing his smiling visage and announcing both that you love *and* hate that darn SOB.

eMpTy RECORDs

po box 12034   seattle, wa   98102

The Journalists Memorial also calls to mind the Tribune Tower in Chicago, where chunks of stone from other world-class piles (the Great Pyramid, the Taj Mahal, the Great Wall of China) stud its fake-Gothic facade and lend world classness to a publication that, in Colonel McCormick's heyday, broke all existing records for abusive boorishness. The masters of *USA Today*, of course, are press lords of a different kind; they preside over a whirling interactive democracy in which The People have long since dispensed with the monoliths of high culture, and their symbolic needs are understandably different. The Gannettoids don't need reminders of Glorious Pastness to sanctify their mission, but a colossal list of names, of martyrs from different faiths, countries, and centuries, all of them rounded up and plunked down a few steps from the USA Today building, as though this were it, as though 30 percent profits, full-color weather maps, a union-free workplace, and nationwide access to the staccato banalities of Al Neuharth were the great causes for which each of them died.

While examining the Journalists Memorial I try to imagine for a minute what goes on here during the day, how the prosperous Gannettoids who inhabit these buildings must come out on this bridge to eat their lunches, how they must sit here next to this monument to the fallen and chew their focaccio and envy each other's company rings and cellphones and subtly rolled collars . . . and then it occurs to me: *It is day*. And yet there

is nobody here. The sky is gray. The street is gray. The building housing the Newseum is gray. No pedestrians walk the streets; no faces peer out from behind the mirrored glass windows of the surrounding office blocks. So fabricated is the landscape that one can't even be sure when, exactly, one stands on terra firma: The people who do occasionally appear walk back and forth on enclosed pedestrian bridges where their tasseled loafers might never encounter the elements; cars creep sporadically in and out of concealed underground parking garages; nearby a concrete church is built over a concrete filling station; and just a few blocks down from the Newseum lurks what must be the world's only underground Safeway, hewn from the solid concrete, its only entrance emptying into yet another parking garage.

It is a curious place for the nation's only monument to journalism's fallen. Why not New York or Chicago, where the frenzied babel of daily journalism gave rise to what little literature we have managed to produce; or at least Detroit, where one of the last great newspaper wars raged until none other than Gannett entered the scene and turned the war on the workers instead? How did it come to pass that this city, whose journalistic contributions have ranged from despicable apologias for the naked exercise of imperial power (Alsop, Pegler) to unspeakable foolishness (George Will, Fred Barnes), is permitted to lay claim to the names of Elijah Lovejoy and Ernie Pyle? Maybe, though, the Journalists Memorial is less a monument than a funeral pyre, a symbolic flame of pink- and orange-colored glass wherein all those dead journalists, those prairie crusaders and abolitionist Jeremiahs, burn now for *USA Today.* Maybe Arlington is where journalism has come to die, in a place as distant as could be found from the urban maelstrom and the rural anger that once nourished it, within easy reach of the caves of state, sunk deep in the pockets of corporate power, here where busloads of glassy-eyed, well-dressed high schoolers from the affluent suburbs of northern Virginia can play anchorman on its grave.

Cordon Sanitaire

Action Pact: *The Punk Singles Collection*
(Captain Oi!, 1995)

Remember roots-rock? The Long
Ryders, Green On Red, and of course Ja-
son and the Nashville Scorchers? Neither
does anybody else. But if Tortoise can make
Spirogyra hip to a new generation of people
with disposable income, you know it's only
a matter of time before every forgotten rock
subgenre becomes somebody's cool her-
metic influence. Except early Eighties British hardcore. This music will *never* be cool.
The aroma of secondhandness sticks to it
like the smell of McDonald's special sauce
on Clinton's trousers. The funny thing is,
this was also true of California hardcore
for a long time. Go back and check out
the *Village Voice*'s music pages from the
early Eighties; Cali and Brit hardcore are
constantly lumped together as the music
of teenage lunkheads, too out of it to realize the action had moved on to the
Mudd Club.

Ten years later, though, something
happened. With the advent of Nirvana
and the mass-marketing of (formerly)
indie rock, Cali hardcore now stood as
the venerable ancestor of the new classic
rock, Robert Johnson to Cobain's Eric
Clapton. The shit was now *canonical*.
Compelled to figure out where this stuff
came from, to set up a *lineage* for it, rock
critics revised their take on hardcore, at
least in its American incarnation. What
had seemed like the frantic scrawlings of
a caged animal now looked like a dia-
gram for genuine rock auteurdom. In a
bizarre final twist to the rehabilitation

of the original, tenth-generation Cali
hardcore itself became a respectable
genre with the success of Green Day,
Offspring, et al. Now we get to read these
retrospective pieces in rock mags and
books about how we all know how *semi-
nal* Black Flag and the Germs were, when
in fact those same canon-makers were
writing stuff well into the Eighties depicting hardcore as *terminal*, the punk
rock equivalent of a rabid mule. Luckily
it couldn't breed, they thought. While
American hardcore led eventually to the
creation of several important industries
(though Puffy's gonna wipe 'em all out
soon) British hardcore led nowhere. The
music retains its stigma as a dead end.
Few critics are willing to appreciate it on
its own terms. (They're not willing to do
that with its early Eighties peers in Cali
either, but that stuff they can look at
through the lens of the stuff it influ-
enced, which is what they really like to
do anyway, which is why everything they
write about it comes off canned.)

What sucks is that the best of this music which has been so blithely written out
of the history books not only rocked like
mad, it also tells us something about the
history of its own time in a way you won't
find anywhere else, tells it so that if you
let yourself into its world you'll never forget it. Its world was the beginning of our
world, the world of neoliberalism and ex-
pendable people. That may have something to do with why Brit hardcore left no
survivors. American hardcore was oriented
toward the personal, almost private angst

of its audience; it conjured an ineffable horror stalking the nation's suburbs, too vague to pin down and too immense to attack directly; it hatched its millennial schemes through the cracks in the walls of anonymous houses, behind dumpsters in the alley, hidden in the tall grass surrounded by chain link fences, occasionally darting out to commit acts of incomprehensible vengeance. It was like the smoke from a fire somewhere off-camera. What We Do Is Secret! As a result, it was left to its own devices for a decade, mutating in a thousand different directions. Brit hardcore, by contrast, saw itself as the vanguard of a young British working class determined to confront the forces of order and defeat them. It drew much of its inspiration from the memory of 1977, when punk appeared to have genuinely spooked respectable folk in a way it never did elsewhere. More relevant, though, was the Brit hardcore generation's own experiences.

When she took office in 1979, Prime Minister Margaret Thatcher enacted brutally stringent fiscal austerity measures to curb inflation and strengthen the position of British finance capital. The unemployment rate skyrocketed, particularly among youth, far beyond even the critically high levels of 1977 immortalized in songs like the Pistols' "Seventeen." Thatcher had known this would happen, and probably thought it would have a salutary effect on the ungrateful little bastards, but they had a surprise for her. A confrontation between skinheads and Pakistani teenagers in South London in the summer of 1981 erupted into a night of youth rioting that left entire city blocks charred and emergency rooms full of wounded cops. No sooner had the fires gone out in London, however, than youth mobs in Manchester attacked the Moss Side police station, leaving nary a stone standing. It went on like that for about a week, spreading through most of Britain's major urban areas: Youth rioting would die down in one city only to explode in another. All told, it was Britain's most severe urban unrest in well over a century. With the exception of the initial South London clash, the rioters directed their fury not at other kids but at the cops and (with varying degrees of explicitness) at those who stood behind them. The rioters were a cross-section of the country's races and subcultures, united by their youth and by the tactical obtuseness of the police, who attacked white and black, punk and Ted alike, thus giving them a common enemy. Brit hardcore songs referred to the riots again and again, as proof of British kids' unity and power, proof of the inevitability of their victory over their common enemy. ("This is our answer/To your laws!" sang the vocalist of the Violators in "Summer of '81," calling out one by one the name of each city scorched by the riots.) Even the pro-Thatcher press thought the Iron Lady was finished.

But now it was the punks' turn to be surprised. Thatcher used the royal wedding of 1981 and the victorious Falklands War of 1982 to drum up patriotic support for her government. The rivers of finance capital conjured up by Thatcher's economic policies generated an economic boom in London and the south of England. At the same time, the economic situation in the North, already seemingly at rock bottom, went from bad to worse to awful beyond belief. British youth split along this regional divide just like everybody else. While London kids flirted with a "New Romanticism" of synthetic luxury, virtually the entire under-25 workforce of Liverpool was unemployed. The Brit hardcore constituency had been dispersed, one half snapping pictures of Duran Duran for *The Face*, the other snapping strangers' necks for a fix. Thatcher's landslide reelection in 1983 just drove the final nail into the movement's coffin; by 1985 it had all but vanished. Brit hardcore drew its power from the conviction that it stood for a united, indomitable community of insurgents; as that community vanished, so did the voice. There were various routes of retreat before the final surrender: bleary-eyed fraternal pub-chants, rural utopianism, formless rage. But a few intrepid souls recorded what was happening to them with that same strange compulsion that makes people stare at twisted bodies in a car wreck. Eventually history disintegrated them along with the rest, but they left these documents behind, and when you listen to them you hear voices calling from a world that no longer exists, warning you about a future which is now your own present. This is what Action Pact was about.

The group formed in London in the riot summer of 1981. The members were all in their teens; singer George (female, name notwithstanding) was all of sixteen. In the fall of that year, they released their first single, the rumbling, generic and altogether wonderful "London Bouncers," which only hinted at the greatness to come but established the leitmotif of Action Pact's music: Instead of looking at "politics" as something abstract and external to your own experience, figure out the larger political significance and implications of the everyday life (in this case the way the "scene" mirrors the very social institutions it was supposed to be fighting against). "Don't accuse me of being petty," snarls George, seemingly anticipating the argument that, with the smoke of the riots still hanging in the air, there were more pressing concerns than London bouncers. With a voice like George's, though, credibility cannot be doubted. I should say something about this voice, perhaps the strangest, most remarkable instrument in Brit hardcore. It stands quite apart from the Pauline Murray-on-crank persona that was the standard mode of the genre's female vocalists (such as the singer from the Expelled, whose single "Dreaming" is still Brit hardcore's most chillingly beautiful moment). It sounds like a speaking voice even when it's carrying a tune, passionate but sensible, with a delightful mocking edge to it; but sometimes George's entire person seems to erupt convulsively, as if she's a bottle with something so volatile inside her that the cork keeps popping off.

The voice was used to even better effect on the band's next single, "Suicide Bag," a rant against glue-sniffing and social despair released in July '82. The song's jagged, white-hot music hits the listener like a chain of explosions—its own kind of testimony to the thrill and power of engagement and anger. The band alternately barrels through a line of roaring power chords like some irresistible force and gets locked into a sputtering, frothing holding action, with George's voice exploding all over the place as she and the band drive the beat through the wall. Erratic, compulsive, uncontainable, "Suicide Bag" radiates the sense of confidence and adventure Brit hardcore kids like Action Pact got from riot summer, the surprise and thrill of discovering their own power. ("Suicide Bag" is also available, along with "Summer of '81" and much else, on *Punk and Disorderly III—The Final Solution* [Anagram, 1994], which also features a hilarious cover collage of bobbies executing punks firing-squad-style in front of 10 Downing Street as Thatcher applauds demurely in the background.)

Even as "Suicide Bag" hit UK turntables, however, the ground was shifting beneath the boots of the Britpunk army. Action Pact's March '83 single "People" captured the growing chill in the air. "There is no such thing as society," Thatcher had so notoriously announced, "only individual men and women." This was the code of the London yuppiedom that Thatcher's policies were generating—a milieu, as it happens, that was attracting many of the London kids punk had claimed to speak for. "People" was Action Pact's reply. The jagged rhythms of "Suicide Bag" are gone, replaced by a steady midtempo throb of thick guitar-bass buzz, relentless and inescapable like a curse. George's voice has gotten steadier, without losing any of its power. When she sings "Tread on those you leave behind," the horror and outrage in her voice cuts through the music like a laser. George wants the proto-yuppie she's talking to to see the invisible human wreckage around him—the cause and consequence of dismissing society. "People! People! People!" she snarls as the band bears down on the chorus, like anything more elaborate would be a capitulation: We are *human*, you bastards, and you'd better treat us as such! This threatening undertone (George warns her target he better be always looking over his shoulder) and the sullen churning rage of the music suggest that resistance is still possible, but the song also tacitly acknowledges that Thatcherism has prevailed.

Two months later Thatcher was re-elected in a landslide. Action Pact's next single, "A Question of Choice," attempted to make sense of what had happened, to find a hole in the net closing in around England and slip away to a place where criticism and action were still possible. Every line ends with a question mark, as if George isn't sure anymore that she can shock people into seeing a thing by sticking it in their face ("People!"); maybe they really *can't* see it, so if not, what *do* they see? As George ticks off the questions her voice drifts back and forth with the melody, flat and conversational. The music is more circumspect, too, patient and precise as it outlines the argument via repetition, the guitar no longer a roar but a steady buzz. George's questions form piece by piece into a picture of the desperate fragmented hopes and fears driving England's strange changes. As her voice gets steadier and stronger you can almost hear her start to smile: I know what this is now, and I know I can talk them out of it. But nobody was listening anymore. By 1984, Brit hardcore bands were breaking up left and right, their records no longer even cracking the indie charts. What should have been Action Pact's last single, "Yet Another Dole Queue Song," is the sound of people who know this may be their last chance to say the words that matter the most, to say something that needs terribly to be heard. The music is still forcebeat guitar-buzz punk rock but it's earnest, even tender, with a guitar lead that flows through the song like an open vein.

I picture the band busking on a street corner in London: People are going home from work, it's nearly evening now and pale blue light is coming down from the sky above the new glass office towers and there's a chill in the air, which is odd because George's face feels hot, and she wonders whether she should go up to one of these passersby and *tell them* this terrible thing, they have to hear it, so she grabs this woman by the arm and says, look, I know you've heard this before a million times and I know how depressing it is, but I have to break the silence, thousands of us, they're taking it all away from us, everything we love, everything we are, and we can't, we can't ignore it much longer, because. . . . The woman wrenches her arm away, gives her this *look*, storms off. George watches people walk past and words start rolling out of her mouth again, she can't help it. You don't think it affects you, right? You think I'm crazy for talking like this, don't you? Listen, they've written off half of the country, do you understand what that means, how awful it is. We can be so much better than this, we used to know how, just three years ago, don't any of you remember? How can you just walk away like this?

Action Pact did release another single, but "Yet Another Dole Queue Song" was really their end, and the end of Brit hardcore as well. Action Pact was unwilling to accept the legitimacy of neoliberalism and its values to *any* extent, thus ensuring their rapid extinction; but they also knew what the new order meant and what kind of future it would bring. When I listen to them it seems to me that music is much poorer, more timid and compromised today for the loss of that crude intransigence.

–Mike O'Flaherty

. . . some little oasis of fatality *amid a wilderness of error . . . .*

—Edgar Allan Poe, "William Wilson"

Poe in Vietnam

I.

Back when I lived in California, I used to travel to Orange County to shop for secondhand books. I followed the same routine each time I went. First, I would drive to the Book Baron at Ball and Magnolia Boulevard in Anaheim, home to about a million volumes. Then I would proceed to the town of Orange, where I would go south on Tustin Street. I frequented three stores on the west side of the street, to my right. One day I happened to look to the left and spotted a secondhand bookstore I hadn't previously seen. I stopped by and looked over the merchandise. Most of the titles were unexceptional and a little overpriced. But one title grabbed my eye among the fiction paperbacks: *The LBJ Brigade*. The name of the author, as given on the spine, was William Wilson. I wondered if that was his real name, or a pseudonym inspired by the well-known Poe story.

The book's cover gave me a bit of a jolt. It featured a painting of a war medal, complete with ribbon. On the face of the medal, rather than an eagle, a sword, or the other standard emblems, was the head of a dead soldier fixed on a bamboo pole, his lips sewn shut. The absence of an ISBN number showed that it was a book from the Sixties, and I figured it dated from 1968 or 1969, when antiwar sentiment was reaching a peak. I checked the copyright page. To my astonishment the book turned out to have been issued—

as a paperback, anyway—in May 1966, a time when the war was still supported by most American citizens and when only a few professors, old and new Leftists, and students ventured to disagree. Furthermore, the name of the original hardbound publisher, "The Apocalypse Corporation," hinted, along with the decapitated GI on the cover, at the nightmarish style that would become the standard vocabulary for literary treatments of the war more than a decade later. The volume was clearly worth picking up at its marked price of thirty cents.

Reading the novel some weeks later, I realized that whoever William Wilson was, his book was as far removed from the common run of war novels—or antiwar novels, for that matter—as humanly imaginable. I decided to do a little research on him at the University of California at Santa Cruz library. I soon determined that he apparently had published one other novel, *Detour,* which I purchased in Palo Alto not long afterward.

Beyond that, I could find little information about Wilson. He was born in 1935, according to the Library of Congress catalog cards for his books. He had two addresses, one on Sunset Drive in L.A., whence Wilson apparently published his first book, and another, the Manhattan address of his agent, given on the copyright page of his second novel. That is all. And that is apparently how Wilson wanted it. Reviewing *The LBJ Brigade* for Carey McWilliams's *Nation,* Joel Lieber (later to write the novel *Move!*, which was made into an Elliott Gould movie, and still later to fatally defenestrate himself) commented that when he wrote to the publishers for information beyond what was on the jacket—"a young American soldier's shocking story of warfare in Vietnam"— he was given no more than that sentence, once again.

The absence of even the sketchiest facts about the novelist's life, naturally, forces attention on the texts themselves. And, indeed, both books are worthy of close attention because, in their savagery, in their hopelessness, in their utterly pitiless view of human society, *The LBJ Brigade* is to the Vietnam novel and the American horror novel what Paul Cain's *Fast One* is to the hard-boiled fiction of the Thirties and Tom Kromer's *Waiting for Nothing* is to the "proletarian" novel of the same decade. But while Cain's and Kromer's novels appeared fairly late in the development of their genres, with styles and themes that could only have been achieved by stripping down previous attempts, Wilson's novel came very early in the history of the genre to which it belongs. In fact, *The LBJ Brigade* could not have been refined from other novels of American combat in Vietnam because there *were none* when it came out.

II.

The first novels about World War I, published while the battle still raged, were modeled after the upbeat tales of adventure, glory, and derring-do made popular in the last century by G. A. Henty and Richard Harding Davis. Not until 1920, in the wake of Versailles, did the first grim exposés of war's futility begin to appear, a literary trend that culminated in 1929 with the international success of *All Quiet on the Western Front*. *A Farewell to Arms*, published the same year, combined that sensibility with a code of fortitude and thus produced what was for many years the reigning model for American war writing. It clearly served, for example, as the

pattern for the first novel of World War II combat published in America—1942's *East of Farewell*, by future Watergate conspirator E. Howard Hunt (though Hunt's subsequent books reverted to the blither style of Henty and Davis). American novels published during the half-decade after the war, like *The Naked and the Dead* and *From Here to Eternity*, updated Hemingway's stoicism by infusing it with the tired, indifferent tone of Bill Mauldin's GI cartoons. It wasn't until the Sixties that novels treating the war in a less realistic style, like Joseph Heller's *Catch-22*, began to appear.

By the same token, almost all the early novels written about Vietnam came in the mold of James Jones or Norman Mailer. *The LBJ Brigade*, alone in the Sixties, prefigures the surrealistic treatment of the war done so effectively by Tim O'Brien in *Going After Cacciato* (1976), even as it surpasses that book in its hallucinatory quality. But William Wilson's status as the first "Vietnam novelist" is a little deceptive: *The LBJ Brigade* is "about" Vietnam in the same way that "Heart Of Darkness" is "about" Belgian colonialism in Africa.

According to the bibliography in Sandra Wittman's *Writing About Vietnam*, of the 400 novels and story collections about the Vietnam War and related events published before 1989, only about a dozen titles predate January 1966. Of these, six are about the French war in Vietnam, focusing on Dien Bien Phu and its immediate aftermath. One is a James Bond ripoff set in Hanoi. Two are romance tales of Army nurses. One concerns CIA activities in Vietnam and Laos in the early Sixties. One was *The Green Berets*, an egregious bit of 1965 gung-hokum that had more in common with Floyd Gibbons's stirring stories of manly valor than with any serious war novel since Henri Barbusse's *Under Fire*. Three are more or less based on the fateful escapades of Cols. Edwin Lansdale and Lucien Conein in the late Fifties and early Sixties: Graham Greene's prophetic *The Quiet American* and William Lederer and Eugene

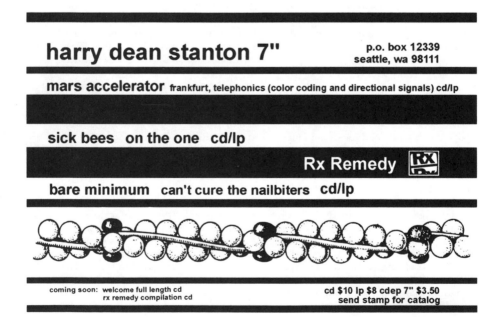

Burdick's two works, *The Ugly American* and *Sarkhan*.

The history of the latter two books may have had some bearing on Wilson's decision to initially self-publish his novel. *The Ugly American,* set in an obvious stand-in for South Vietnam called "Sarkhan"; it was a national bestseller in 1958, was later made into a movie starring Marlon Brando, and probably contributed in no small degree to the initial reluctance of American opinion to sanction military action in Vietnam beyond the presence of a few thousand "advisors." Some years later its authors wrote a sequel. But problems developed. The initial publisher pulled out of the deal. Lederer and Burdick managed to place *Sarkhan* with another house, but even then the book, despite some good reviews, failed to appear in a number of bookstores and terminated their string of successes. The two believed that federal pressure had been applied to keep the book from having the impact of their previous efforts.

The was the milieu in which someone, identifying himself by the title of Poe's tale of the *doppelgänger*, chose to publish his extraordinary novel.

III.

R. Z. Sheppard, who wrote the first review of *The LBJ Brigade* for the *New York Herald Tribune* in February 1966, found the novel shocking. The cover illustration in particular, he pointed out, caused a "reaction . . . strangely similar to the momentary disbelief I experienced a few months ago when I opened the newspaper to a photograph of [President Johnson] displaying his gall-bladder scar."

The book retains a good deal of this power to disturb. It is composed entirely in the first-person present tense, and is related by a narrator with no name. Although the present tense has been used to lend "immediacy" to a vast range of mediocre novels over the last twenty years, it seems almost mandatory here.

It opens with what seems to be a scene from a Frankie and Annette beach-party movie, and images from this vision flicker incongruously through the narrator's head almost up to his grisly end. It is phrased as a sort of incantation, in its odd way bringing to mind both Lautréamont's command that the reader of *Maldoror* close the pages at once before it is too late, and his assertion in *Poésies* that school prize-giving speeches are the highest form of literature:

I am 1-A.

1-A is the national seal of approval, it means that I am the cream of American manhood.

I am 1-A, there is a war in Southeast Asia, the President says, "We are in Vietnam to fulfill one of the most solemn pledges of the American nation."

This is immediately followed by:

It is summer and the Sunday beaches are crowded. We swim and sing, and some glide the phosphorescent crowns of wild breakers carrying cans of beer above their heads. The girls have blue eyes and green, with frames of dark paint, and they cheer and dig at the hot sand with coy toes . . . . Our bodies are wet with sun and greased with oils, and we are overcome with childish delight.

Childish delight, that is, which must nonetheless be defended: "A young man should have a few adventures before he settles down," the narrator observes, preparing to move from the world of *Beach Blanket Bingo* to that of, perhaps, *The Wackiest Ship in the Army*.

He is inducted in Los Angeles, and then takes the train for Oakland before sailing overseas. When he reaches Oakland, however:

Crowds begin to appear on street corners, this is more like it, the people are out to wave and shout. But we find that they are not people, they are Communists and pacifists, they hold signs, STOP THE WAR IN VIETNAM, they have come to sit in front of the train to stop the war in Vietnam, most of them are young, college-age, they wear expensive clothes. . . . We wave and the kids wave and yell back, everybody is having a good time, but we are going to war and they are standing in the streets breaking laws and getting free publicity, the government should draft them all, that is the only way to treat them.

Two things are worth noting here. *They wear expensive clothes.* Most other novelists treating this subject would go on for pages about the class structure of the draft, the bourgeois background of the protesters, etc. But for Wilson, those four words will do. *They are not people.* This lets the careful reader know early on in which direction the narrator's thoughts will proceed, but this is not something I picked up in my first reading. A 1967 reviewer noted Wilson's style of "nervous anguish," and we can detect the beginnings of this beneath the narrator's still-intact bravado. As the book progresses these two opposed tendencies will become better and better defined, alternately rising to the surface of the narrator's consciousness and disappearing. But what makes Wilson's treatment of them remarkable (and also prescient) is the way in which the rhetoric of bravado eventually becomes inseparable from that of anguish.

The next paragraph opens: "The Vietnam countryside is calm and serene." Three paragraphs later: "Corporal Cohn is dead," accidentally shot when returning from patrol. "I do not even know his first name," the narrator remarks—not that the first names of any of the other soldiers are ever given, either. (Meanwhile, the narrator's scattered memories of "the girls back home" include first names only, beach-movie names like Joan, Donna, Brooke, and Lynn.)

In the next section, the reader meets Sergeant Sace, who announces, simply, that "I been here for ten years. [That is, since Dien Bien Phu.] I'm still alive."

> "You're gonna have ta kill some people. Ya best get used ta the idea." He talks but we do not learn anything. He knows it. He ends by saying, "This's all bullshit, ya gotta learn it the hard way."

Before the soldiers learn it that way, however, they make each other's acquaintance: Corporals Smith, Ames, Handson, Maria, Banner. Captain Shine is their officer. We learn that Shine is a bit of a martinet, Banner is black, Smith is "a bigot from Arkansas" who nonetheless is not mean when he drinks, and that Corporal Handson, the only college man in the brigade except the narrator, is already skeptical about the war, asserting every day: "The government kidnapped me." When Handson remarks, *"La guerre sans fronts,"* Corporal Ames muses: "He's a spy, he speaks Communist."

The men head out on patrol, and before long are burning a village and beating up some teenagers. Sergeant Sace warns: "Don't touch nothin', the little bastards'll boobytrap turds." For the moment, no one is killed. Then they are back in Saigon, and the narrator editorializes for a few terse pages about a behind-the-lines situation that filled books for other writers:

> Our folks taught us that liquor and cursing and pimps and narcotics and thieves and whores are evil, and they have sent us right to these very things, to a summer-camp of sin. Our folks are angry. And Vietnam, Vietnam is angry,

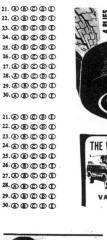

Hunter Kennedy

because we are turning their daughters into whores. But we are close to war and death, we are risking our lives for their goddam country, the least they can do is provide some free ass.

Eventually the soldiers reach a bar where they encounter a well-dressed American reporter. The tone of the conversation that ensues, in which the various characters ruminate about the war and its goals in tones ranging from the cynical to the tiredly defensive, has since become a cliché of Vietnam writing and Vietnam film. But this was published in the first weeks of 1966, and the device here makes its very first appearance. The reporter asks the men if they are glad to be doing what they do. "We're here to stop Communists," the still-idealistic narrator asserts. Handson, the college-educated doubter, asserts that "this is genocide, not war."

I'm fighting so that my family can live in freedom. Shit. My family lives in a thirty-thousand dollar tract house. My mother worries about losing her freedom about as much as she does about growing a third tit.

Sergeant Sace, dismayed by the scarcity of whores in the bar, offers this view of how it, and perhaps all of Vietnam, should be handled: "We oughta Hiroshima the whole joint." The reporter, a latter-day disciple of Richard Harding Davis, is displeased with these responses. When Handson says of LBJ that "he's giving a whole new meaning to the 'I' pronoun," that the president is "the Christ of mediocrity," the journalist yells, "Jesus, buddy, whose side you on?" After years of hearing about the perfidy of the media in Vietnam, contemporary readers may find it hard to believe that journalists were capable of such blind loyalty, but such was the case, especially in the earliest days of the conflict. (Some of these journalists later moved into the "dove" camp in spectacular fashion.)

The next day the men go on a search-and-destroy mission and are landed right into an ambush. Within seconds of stepping out of their helicopter all of them except the narrator and Sace are killed. Wilson's lingering descriptions of each man's end bring to mind the "magic realism" of the Latin American novel—hallucinatory and yet all too accurate. Captain Shine is the first to go:

"I'm shot," he tells Banner. "I'm shot!" he yells. "I'm shot!" he screams. He sits down, comically, his legs snap out and he falls heavily on his buttocks, he crosses his arms on his chest, leans back, his head thumps the ground. He says, "Momma," and is dead.

"Ames disintegrates like a glass house, he rains back into the weeds," Wilson writes, reminding us what happens to people who throw stones out of turn. Then "the right side of [Banner's] face explodes." A soldier named Stein goes next:

[T]here are a dozen bullets in him before he screams, "Don't let me die, don't let me die, please don't let me die!" It is a death-chant, the notes run down the scale.

Handson, the antiwar character, puts his gun to his own head and curses God—the sin which became such a familiar trope in subsequent antiwar books and movies—just as a sniper's bullet finishes him. All the while, "The rifle in my hands softly kicks, but it is like trying to kill an ocean. You can't kill jungle, fella," the narrator remarks to himself. This image, too—technology's futility against vast, chaotic nature—would soon become standard in writing about the conflict. Nonetheless, he and Sace manage to survive.

So there they are, Dante and his profane Virgil, in their green inferno. Army choppers show up, and the narrator, overjoyed, is ready to signal them. Sace shoves him down and the choppers strafe the ground with fire meant to kill Vietcong who have already left. As the two men slowly move out, Sace gives an explanation of war that at first repulses the narrator:

"Screw what ya been told in the States. Ya ain't fightin the Communists, ya ain't fightin Charlie. Ya ain't fightin for liberty or America or the cunt next door. You're fightin ta stay alive. If you wanna live, ya gotta kill. . . . Ya ain't gonna have no trouble knowin who ta shoot. If he ain't white, shoot em. This's a race-war kid. A hundred-year-old hag can kill ya just as dead as a hot Charlie. So can a ten-year-old kid. If he ain't white, screw the question, shoot. . . . The Arvin [South Vietnamese soldier] can throw away his uniform and he's one a the crowd, but not you. You're white, un the white man's a target."

"But it's wrong!"

He leaps up, he yells, "Ya get that crap out a your head!"

Putting his words into practice, Sace mows down two men in uniform along with a woman. The narrator is repulsed as he contemplates the dead Vietnamese but it is clear that he has already begun to move closer to Sace's thinking. The men are becoming spiritual doubles in the manner of Poe's story "William Wilson":

Large wet dents show the concentrated impact on the man and woman, but the last man's face is pulped, the head half ripped from the neck. There is a sickening and sad odor at the end of living when that end is violent, it is the embarassing odor of fertilizer. The girl's breasts are exposed, one is round, still flushed, the nipple extended and rigid as though excited, but the other is slashed, like a lid it hangs down on her stomach. Her cheekbones are long and wide, they dimple her cheeks with large half-moons of baby flesh, she should not be dead, she should be alive, we should have captured her, she would rather be my slave the rest of her life than dead, she would be thankful, she would cherish and love me.

But before many pages have passed, Sace, too, has been killed, leaving the narrator to wander Vietnam with only his murderous hallucinations. At one point he mows down eight villagers on a jungle path. Almost ludicrously evoking the language of the Dick and Jane primer, he muses: "See? See, the bodies are dead. On the path the bodies are

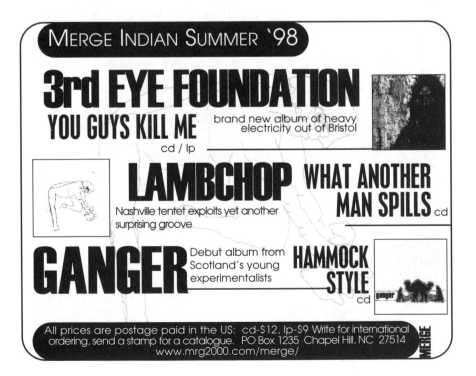

dead, poor bodies. See the poor dead bodies." But a moment later he switches gears to an equally childish triumphalism: "The Communists are dead, they are all dead, I have killed the Communists, now they cannot hurt America, now America is safe, I have saved America."

The narrator then enters a village that is instantly gassed by American planes, causing the villagers to choke, vomit, and "die of fear." But Peter Arnett may rest assured that a tear-gas attack is what is being described, since the narrator lives and is taken prisoner by a Vietcong officer named Vo Chi Diem who passes the time reciting Radio Hanoi boilerplate.

With plenty of time to meditate on Sace's "kill or be killed" philosophy, the narrator now begins to spin his own variation of it. "All these guys know is that the white man dropped the bomb on the colored man," Sace had told the narrator; the "colored" people surrounding him in the bush want only to get back for it by killing him; ergo, his job is to kill them first. The crude sergeant had not been interested in ideology, countries, or governments. But the narrator, being an educated man, begins to put Sace's homicidal racism in precisely the political terms that Sace warned him against, transforming it into the megalomania of a rampant, pretentious fascism:

> We must rid the world of all the Communists, we cannot go half way, we have to go all the way, we cannot kill just some of them, they are not all evil but we cannot take any chances, a Communist is a Communist, they all look alike. Hitler had the same problem with the Jews, he did not kill them all and he failed, when free men fight for the survival of mankind they cannot take chances. . . . We must act before it is too late, we must kill them all, every last one, even the children, children grow up into Communists.

Moments later, as dusk falls, the narrator changes his tone entirely. Now he is penitent and fearful: "I didn't mean anything, really, I didn't do it on pur-

pose, I'm sorry, I'm sorry." But then a titanic air attack, powerful enough to put a dent into the vastness of nature, annihilates his Vietnamese escorts:

> A block-wide section of jungle collapses into itself, then squirts out like a fist smashing down on a cube of jello. Greenery is pulverized, it splashes like water, trees catapult upward trailing long tails of bush and vine. . . .

Feeling "something" approach his prostrate form, the narrator lapses into a final burst of megalomania:

> It thinks it can trick me. I cannot be tricked. I cannot be harmed. I laugh, exaltation blazes, I am God, I am the American Dream, I am Mars. It senses my rage, it perceives the destruction I create in the heart of the universe, it raises the knife, it feels and hears the death I bring to the enemies of America and of God, it swings, it swings, too late, the air hums and turns to fire, the world shudders, the ground dissolves, trees explode, the earth bursts, I

And on that pronoun *The LBJ Brigade* ends.

"What is most effective about the book is that the ending is unexpected," noted the *Times Literary Supplement* reviewer. "We expect that the narrator will see the futility of the war. He doesn't." Instead, the narrator practically articulates Lieutenant Calley's defense of his role in the My Lai massacre—*They were all the enemy. They were all to be destroyed*—more than two years before that massacre occurred.

"Obviously, the book can be read as propaganda," the *TLS* continued, "but it deserves discussion as vision rather than argument because Mr. Wilson persuades us that he is more concerned to explore feelings than merely to attack American policies." Indeed, much of the book's power derives from its refusal to conform to the established patterns of the war novel. The captain may be a martinet, but he is not the coward familiar from so many books penned by enlisted men; he leads the men out of the chopper and is the first to die. The sergeant enters the story straight from

The Sands of Iwo Jima, but then becomes more recognizably human as the narrator far surpasses him in bigotry and craven monstrosity. For all its blood and bullets, the book's lesson is subtle and subjective rather than openly argued: Vietnam is making us into fascists. The only real contemporary parallel to *The LBJ Brigade*, the one creative work of the mid-Sixties that most brings to mind its combination of terror, crude humor, mindless longing for home, and what one reviewer called a "jumping muscularity," is not a book but an album made in Germany by five former GIs in tonsures: the Monks' *Black Monk Time*, reissued last year on American Recordings.

Since his second novel, *Detour*, Wilson has never published again, and perhaps with reason. His critique of the darker side of American aspirations, embedding his strange social theory in a gruesomeness more advanced than that of Bret Easton Ellis, seems more like the stuff of Aeschylus or Euripides than of David Cronenberg or Wes Craven. Wilson's constant theme—that American efforts to purify or escape the corruptions

of civilization merely substitute one corruption for another—hearkens back to *Edgar Huntly, Arthur Gordon Pym, Moby Dick,* and, of course, "Heart Of Darkness." Today the idea has gone stale, rehashed again and again in films like *Platoon* and *Apocalypse Now.* But there is a difference: Wilson's books never offer us even the small shreds of hope that these otherwise dark films insist on holding out. In *Platoon,* for example, Oliver Stone pits a soldier of decency and sweetness against one of unalloyed viciousness and evil in a battle for the soul of Charlie Sheen: the two cancel each other out. But for Wilson there is only Sace's repulsive but undeniably *authentic* view of the Vietnamese and what to do with them—"authentic" in the Greek sense, referring to a murderer who does not shirk from admitting the nature of his actions—and the narrator's repulsive but *inauthentic* version, larded with patriotism and anticommunism. Only to the extent that the narrator echoes Kurtz's call to "exterminate all the brutes" does he express something heartfelt; and, unlike Kurtz, he insists on garbing his sentiments in imperial rhetoric to the end.

Continued from page 84

Fairmont Village

171st Pl. & Pembroke   5-9   1:36 PM
Report of group of subjects out at retention pond near McCarthy Park attempting to relocate some fish, park district security notified.

7700 block 170th Pl.   5-17   10:17 AM
Report that persons unknown took pirate's flag from child's playhouse.

7600 block 170th St.   5-20   4:08 PM
Report that resident was pushed over while on his motor scooter.

Tinley Heights

7300 block Dorothy Ln.   5-16   2:14 AM
Complaint of teens in garage playing loud music, advised.

17000 block Ozark   5-26   10:15 AM
2 carloads of teens parked in middle of street, GOA.

7300 block Dorothy   5-28   11:54 AM
Resident reported that handgun was stolen from residence, possibly taken by a family member, case under investigation.

7400 block Dorothy   5-29   9:49 PM
Complaint of kids throwing golf balls at residence.

Brementowne Single Family Homes

St. Julie Church   5-1   7:26 PM
Complaint of juveniles new Activity Center, juveniles dispersed.

Veterans' Park   5-5   5:44 PM
Report of 2 male juveniles sitting at picnic table, appear to be carving something in to benches; park security notified, no apparent damage.

165th & 76th Ave.   5-7   4:20 PM
Report of kids walking with raft, GOA.

16400 block Olcott   5-9   4:24 PM
Male subject walking and trying to sell resident things and looking in his garage; per officer, was solicitor without permit, advised to leave area.

163rd St. & Ozark   5-9   9:16 PM
Report of 2 young teens wrestling on ground, possibly fighting; no problem, were just playing around.

St. Julie Church   5-11   6:51 PM
Employee would like a few skateboarders shagged.

St. Julie Church   5-14   6:53 PM
Complaint of kids on skateboards, shagged.

7500 block 163rd Pl.   5-15   7:12 PM
Resident reported 4 male and 1 female subject came to house threatening to kill son, located, settled by officer.

16500 block 76th Ave.   5-16   12:27 AM
Resident reported unknown subject left dirty socks in his mailbox.

166th Pl. & Bristol Ln.   5-24   7:03 PM
Complaint of kids in street playing croquet, hitting balls toward cars, located and advised.

Brementowne Condominiums

7900 block 163rd Ct.   5-23   3:58 PM
Report of a race car doing "burnouts" in parking lot, owner located and warned.

Timbers Edge

8800 block 172nd St.   5-5   2:51 PM
Complaint of 4-5 juveniles in resident's yard throwing her landscape rocks at her cat, youths located, returned to clean up property and apologized to homeowner.

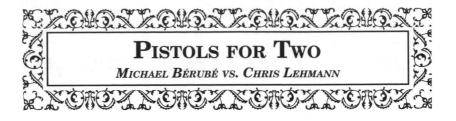

Michael Bérubé Writes:

Flipping through a copy of THE BAF-FLER Number Nine, expecting to be entertained as usual, what do I come across but a hyperbolic, smug, snotty little essay about how all professors are wealthy, self-serving careerists who wouldn't know a class struggle if it bit them on their amply padded asses. The essay opens by citing the he-man left's favorite gadfly, Russell Jacoby, as if Jacoby were some kind of working-class hero instead of a wannabe who's made a career out of mocking academics (after having failed to land an academic job himself) and advocating a return to class politics (which he himself never manages to practice). The essay goes on in a Jacobyan vein for some pages, making plenty of good solid points about the corporate academy that the academic left has already made many times over, and sure enough, making them at the academic left's expense. And by the time I get to the essay's hilarious description of me as "one of the most enthusiastic epigones of critspeak as revolutionary praxis," I figure the author just has to be ol' Jacko himself: No other writer on the planet has been so delusional as to try to pass off this crap as a characterization of me and my work. (Luxury cruises will be awarded to the first person who can find a single sentence I have ever written that justifies either the "critspeak" part or the "revolutionary praxis" part. Readers who can find a single *phrase* will win fabulous discounts on all my books.)

You can imagine my surprise when I got back to the title page and realized that the author was one Chris Lehmann—not Jacoby, it turns out, but an amazing simulation. Well, at least Jacoby treats me with hauteur and disdain largely because he's so pissed that I get invited to write for general-readership lefty journals more often than he does; what the hell, I wonder, can be Lehmann's excuse?

My curiosity now piqued, I read further that my account of the Yale graduate student strike of 1995-96 is "wildly misguided," full of "blindspots" that testify to the "notorious academic misapprehension of 'real world' relations of power," and jeez, I begin to wonder whether Lehmann was the gangly kid whose dog I hit repeatedly with my car a few months ago. At one point, Lehmann grudgingly credits me with having criticized Yale's faculty for breaking the graduate student union's (GESO) grade strike; but then, apparently working on the belief that he is much smarter than any of us mortals, he goes on to point out that I am really, really dumb: "[Bérubé] can never bring himself to supply the simplest explanation for the intransigence of Yale's trustees and administration in the GESO campaign: No private school in America has recognized a graduate student union."

Well, I'll be a monkey's butt. A *private school*, you say? Damn, I wish *I'd* thought of that. Now, why didn't this occur to me? Because, for one thing, I wasn't answering so simple a question

MICHAEL BÉRUBÉ is a professor of English at the University of Illinois at Urbana-Champaign.

CHRIS LEHMANN is an editor at *Newsday*.

as "why did Yale's trustees and administration oppose GESO?" I was asking why Yale's *faculty* overwhelmingly opposed GESO, and why they took such extraordinary (and illegal) measures to do so even though they had no financial stake in the outcome of the dispute. Lehmann insists that the class conflict is the only explanation; but this is not only too simplistic to count as an analysis of university labor disputes, it also (more crucially) makes nonsense of Lehmann's own conclusion that faculty should organize with other workers of their class. OK, that's one thing. For another thing, Yale's status as a private university does not exempt it from federal antidiscrimination laws, and should not exempt it from federal labor law either; in hauling out the "private university" defense, Lehmann has unwittingly toed the line drawn by the Yale Corporation, instead of the much saner NLRB ruling of November 1996 (which Lehmann cites but seems not to have read), or the AAUP resolution of December 1995, both of which grant to all graduate students the right to organize in order to bargain collectively with universities.

Lehmann claims that my essay attributes the Yale crisis to *"sui generis* management styles" and Yale's "generalized institutional culture of 'elitism,' " and therefore faults me (and others ostensibly like me) for substituting "culture" for "class," for failing to see any structural relation between Yale and other schools, for contributing to the demise of the American intellectual left, for padding my C.V., and who knows, maybe for depleting the earth's ozone layer to boot. (In *reality*, by the bye, I did not treat Yale as a unique phenomenon. My essay actually attributed the bullheadedness of Yale faculty to the fact "that they cannot see any structural relation between Yale and the vast legions of lesser American schools"; I opened the essay by talking about unionization at the University of Kansas, and closed it by criticizing a recent MLA president's plan to create "postdocs" that would establish a per-

manent second-tier class of underemployed Ph.D.'s nationwide. In the course of linking the Yale crisis to broader national conditions and the "adjunctification" of university teaching, I did, however, note that Yale has its own specific history of union-busting and unfair labor practices—a history that Chris Lehmann would do well to study.) But allow me, for now, to dodge Lehmann's numerous petty insults, his grandstanding, his off-key paraphrases of my essay. Let's cut to the chase. What is to be done? My argument is that graduate students are also teachers, and that all teachers should have the right to form teacher's unions and bargain collectively. I've made that case not only in the pages of *Social Text* (Lehmann snidely insinuates that my colleagues and I wrote these essays merely to advance our careers) but on campuses across the country, including my own, where my administration is engaged in a costly and foolish struggle to deny recognition to our own graduate student union. In this context, organizing around "class" oppression, as Lehmann suggests, is ludicrous: You'll only pit distinguished chairs against teaching assistants and replicate the Yale scenario nationwide. The answer, instead, lies in good old-fashioned trade unionism. And if you don't trust me on this one, on the grounds that I'm an epigone of any number of rank stupidities, you can take it from Jon Wiener, whose essay in the most recent issue of *Dissent* says the same thing.

On the importance of trade unionism and alliance-building Lehmann and I are pretty much in agreement, which is one reason his general snottiness is so annoying. But there are two more problems with Lehmann's analysis, and taken together, they're fatal. One has to do with the academy, the other with labor. Let's take them in that order.

Problem number one has to do with enrollments in the humanities and the social significance of the academic left. Lehmann insists time and again that the academic left is irrelevant not only to contemporary labor struggles but to everything under the sun, including the socially critical functions of universities. He purchases this point first by citing Jacoby to the effect that one-quarter of all undergraduate degrees go to business majors whereas only 12,000 go to foreign language majors and 7,000 to students in philosophy and religion; and second, by insisting that there has been "an arresting sea change in the last generation of college students: Liberal-arts majors now comprise just 30 percent of all bachelor's degrees awarded nationwide, down from 70 percent in 1970." The problem with this argument is that, like Jacoby, Lehmann tends to run out and play before he's finished his homework. There has indeed been a notable decline in liberal arts degrees since 1970, but the decline occurred almost entirely between the years of 1970 and 1976. Comparing degrees awarded in 1970 with those awarded in 1995 suggests a slow, gradual decline, whereas in fact what happened was more complicated: a plunge in the Seventies, a trough from 1976-1986, then a dramatic rebound in the late Eighties and early Nineties, with the peak of the rebound occurring somewhere around 1993-95. Likewise, comparing current business majors with philosophy, religion, or foreign language B.A.'s, as Jacoby does, is tendentious and misleading—like comparing galaxies to solar systems in order to prove that the latter are insignificant. In 1995, for instance, although business management awarded 234,323 degrees, the behavioral and social sciences as a whole awarded 200,237, and the humanities *as a whole* awarded 192,317. These figures come from the National Center for Education Statistics, which also reports that B.A.'s in English accounted for 7.12 percent of all degrees awarded in 1970, 7.21 percent in 1972, 5.77 percent in 1974, and 4.54 percent in 1976. In 1986 and 1988, by contrast, English B.A.'s comprised 3.5 and 3.89 percent of all degrees; in 1994 and 1995, 4.61 and 4.47 percent.

Why does this barrage of statistics matter to the argument? Because when Andrew Ross attributes the recent downsizing of humanities departments to the rightward shift in national poli-

tics, Lehmann archly accuses Ross of "preening" and "prattling," and claims that humanists are being struck by the budget ax simply because they "preside over departments with declining enrollments." Chris, my boy, this is poppycock. In these United States, the humanities and social sciences awarded 29.5 percent of the nation's 935,140 undergraduate degrees in 1980-81, and 33.9 percent of 1,158,567 undergraduate degrees in 1994-95—an increase in both relative and absolute terms. More telling still: In the past ten years, during which the "downsizing" of humanities departments has accelerated precipitously (and the number of part-time faculty increased from 36 percent to over 45 percent of the profession), bachelor's degrees in history rose 73 percent, in religion and philosophy 31 percent, and in English 71 percent. So the next time someone tries to tell you that downsizing is tied to a drop in enrollment figures, you can either cite these handy statistics or use the even handier one-word rebuttal, "bullshit." Meanwhile, at the University of Illinois, which is a perfectly representative institution in this respect, the College of Liberal Arts and Sciences does 43 percent of the undergraduate teaching but receives only 28 percent of the budget allocations. At no point in recent years, in fact, have funding levels for the humanities matched the student demand for courses in the liberal arts.

What all this means is that if Lehmann really wants to talk about why programs in the humanities are being "right-sized" and eliminated, he's going to have to think about cultural politics (wipe that smirk off your face, young man), and he's going to have to stay in his room a bit longer and finish that nasty homework of his. In the liberal arts, our enrollments have held steady or increased since Gerald Ford left the White House. And as for that precipitous dip in 1970-76: yes indeed, it was caused by the rise of professional schools—and partly (as Francis Oakley pointed out some years ago) by the exodus of undergraduate women from the humanities into pre-law and pre-med programs. Hardly a development worth lamenting, unless you're Pat Robertson.

So much for Lehmann's understanding of the academy. As for labor, let me be brief: When Lehmann proclaims that "if the academy is serious about embracing the agenda of labor, it should do so on labor's terms," I have to wonder how much the lad knows about our labor history. The UAW, for instance, is not a very good model for teachers' unions to follow; neither, for that matter, was the AFT under the neocon leadership of Albert Shanker. The UAW has been a subsidiary of management for decades; the AFT was on the wrong side of the community control movement in New York in 1968 and fought against progressive reforms for the rest of Shanker's reign (which is why, in an old labor house like the one I grew up in, "to shanker" is an irregular verb meaning "to kill progressive reforms"). Had Lehmann been paying attention during the Columbia teach-in, he would have heard that labor and intellectuals split in the Sixties over the Vietnam War. Is Lehmann now endorsing labor's support of that war? And surely I needn't belabor the history of corruption in the pre Carey Teamsters or the sorry AFL-CIO leadership of the pre-Sweeney days of Lane Kirkland. The interesting thing about the recent attempt at a rapprochement between labor and intellectuals, then, is precisely that *both* sides have a lot of sorry history to answer for—and a lot to learn.

Lehmann closes his screed by wagging his finger at us nutty professors and solemnly cautioning us that "solidarity begins at home." Yeah, well, Casey Jones couldn'ta said it better. It's clear to someone like me, who was walking picket lines at St. John's University as soon as he *could* walk, that Lehmann didn't bring to the table a decent understanding of academic labor disputes, or academe, or labor history, or labor unions—just a penchant for sneering at leftist professors, and a smattering of second-hand dogmatic wisdom. Lehmann's article has its decent moments, but even those are marred by his opportunistic tendency to blame people for not writing about events (like the crises at Adelphi or Arizona International University) before they occurred, and his truly bizarre insistence that the *Social Text* contributors should have "shift[ed] their gaze from the elite precincts of a place like Yale"—even though many of the contributors were Yale graduate students. Since THE BAFFLER is pretty good at skewering ersatz "alternative" culture, let me put it this way: The day a Chris Lehmann gets to posture as more savvy and class-conscious that people like Rick Wolff and Robin D.G. Kelley (fellow contributors to *Social Text*) is the day Scott Weiland gets to proclaim himself the godfather of punk. You smart fellows want to write about labor and intellectuals? Then drop the poses and get serious. I know THE BAFFLER can do better—and often enough, it actually does.

Chris Lehmann replies:

What *was* I thinking? Here I had criticized Michael Bérubé for his tendency to personalize the labor conflict at Yale, only to learn that I'm a snotty, gangly kid understudy of a he-man lefty academic wannabe.

I also learn that I maliciously bend statistics to serve the evil designs of Albert Shanker and Pat Robertson, and that I quite possibly supported the Vietnam War, to boot. Gangly but bloodthirsty—a veritable Tony Perkins of left cultural criticism. Imagine the unutterable shame of my parents.

But through the ungainly invective, Bérubé is trying to topple a couple of key points in my BAFFLER essay, so permit me to restrain my snotty urges—down, spiteful pen, *down!*—and address a few of his more substantive complaints. First, the painstaking numbers game: I am being assailed for a 1970 to 1995 comparison; yet my claim that humanities enrollments are declining is trumped by a comparison of 1980 and 1994 figures. Thus we learn that, depending on your points of departure and arrival, numbers are fungible things. Still, the remarkable reversal I mentioned remains, as far as I can see, a remarkable reversal—and I did say that it took place *over a generation*. Nor is it especially unfeminist to note that an enormous influx of professional and preprofessional students, regardless of their gender, continues to transform the university into a full-on bazaar of business culture. (Indeed, it's a rather striking oversimplification to depict women—the largest demographic grouping on the planet—as a univocal progressive interest group, but we'll save that point for another letter.)

There's also the small matter of me (citing my dread svengali, Russell Jacoby) including a comparison of the rather anemic number of degrees granted in undergrad philosophy, religion and foreign language departments with the bulging figures in business schools. Yet to play off behavioral and social sciences against business enrollments, as Bérubé proposes, creates new galaxies of confusion. We know, for example, that sociology—once a proud discipline of astringent social criticism—is being banished from many campuses altogether. Likewise, the term "behavioral and social sciences" is being used to cover ever broader swaths of business-minded specialties such as industrial psychology, public relations, and corporate anthropology. And, as I noted in my essay, more traditional social science disciplines such as political science and economics are being rapidly overtaken by "rational choice," market-based models of inquiry, with predictable implications for the university's culture of would-be dissent. (Meanwhile, Bérubé's complaint about the unfitness of the philosophy and religion comparison becomes especially droll when we read on to see the new upsurge in humanities enrollments that he cites is caused in part by increases in those very same, suddenly no longer quite so unrepresentative, disciplines of philosophy and religion.)

As for those increases: Bérubé insists upon beginning his analysis at the point where the numbers bottomed out—the grim academic season of 1980-81—thus yielding the "increase in both relative and absolute terms" in the awarding of humanities and social science degrees that, he claims, has taken place since. Here I must admit to a certain exegetical glee: After his solemn chiding that the long-term decline in liberal-arts degrees is so much more "complicated" than my numbers had indicated, Bérubé has seen fit to ignore that in both 1993-94 and 1994-95 (the most recent years tabulated by the Department of Education), humanities and social science programs registered small but significant across-the-board *declines*—in English, social sciences and history, foreign languages and literature, and of course, the long-suffering fields of philosophy and religion. "Michael, my boy," I am tempted to write, "you are blowing so much empirical smoke here," but I dunno, that'd be kind of, well, snide, wouldn't it?

But enough bean-counting. The reason such numbers matter, as Bérubé rightly notes, is that many left professors love to portray themselves as an embattled cultural vanguard, nobly fending off all manner of surly right-wing *autos-da-fé*. Andrew Ross is pleased to call this condition "an acute political siege"—and it is from the front-line tents of the culture wars that today's left professors issue their counsel to the benighted workers yearning to be free, on campus and off.

With this broad area of agreement in mind, let's move on to Bérubé's other objections. To begin with his most plausible complaint: It's true that I made no mention of Bérubé's efforts to explain the hostility of Yale faculty to the GESO organizing drive, since, well, such efforts seem rather superfluous. Anyone with a passing acquaintance with labor conflicts can surmise rather quickly that one reason Yale professors resist efforts to improve the sweated conditions of graduate and adjunct instruction is that *they directly benefit from such conditions*. Oh, cripes, there I go again with that oversimplified class analysis—it's almost as bad as Tourette's.

As for the private university question, Bérubé must have been so blinded by visions of a cackling Russell Jacoby that he overlooked this sentence in my piece: "Bérubé is aware of the gap between the successful organizing drives at public universities and the bitterly stalemated ones at Yale." I then noted he largely attributed the obduracy of the struggle to the "elitist" attitudes of Yale faculty and administration. I never endorsed Yale's private-university "defense" of its union-busting; I merely said that it was a more compelling explanation of the university's hard-line stand than the cultural posture of elitism. One might just as reasonably argue that historians of the Old South "toe the line" of the Southern planters' ideological justification of slavery.

As for urging that organizing on campuses proceed on the labor movement's own terms, I cited two specific examples of union activism in the realm of culture and education. I no more suggested that union-minded academics sign on with Albert Shanker's AFT or George Meany's Vietnam War than I suggested they endorse the 1939 Nazi-Soviet pact. This sort of generation-baiting—the notion that the New Left and its latter-day apologists basically own the copyright to political dissent—was one of the things I meant to criticize in the essay, and Bérubé's thundering rhetorical efforts to tar me with retrograde Sixties-era political positions are, it seems to me, a particularly shameful instance of it.

Just out of curiosity, though: What was the "right side" in the 1968 United Federation of Teachers fracas over community control in Ocean Hill-Brownsville? Would that be the side that appointed the breathtakingly unqualified Herman Ferguson—then under indictment (and later convicted) for a plot to assassinate NAACP leader Roy Wilkins—to the community control district's governing board? The side that brought on the Congress of Racial Equality's self-styled "terrorist" (and later Tawana Brawley thug) Sonny Carson to organize paramilitary task forces, sporting helmets and bandoliers

of bullets, to prevent union teachers returning to their jobs—after the Board of Education and the UFT had already brokered a deal to protect both the teachers' contract and the community-control experiment? The side that threatened to send each returning teacher home in a pine box? The side that reneged on a long series of public agreements so as to force a "confrontation" with a "sick society" practicing "educational genocide"? It's true that Albert Shanker became an unsightly neocon during his long tenure at the AFT, but to assert that his principal political failing was being on "the wrong side" of that particular struggle strikes me as a tad, well, simplistic.

But it's more interesting to note what Bérubé *doesn't* attack in my essay. I quite explicitly suggested that, in view of the academy's growing strategy of casualizing its pedagogical workforce, sympathetic professors could embark on a serious rethinking of the institution of tenure and re-examine the corporate-structured system of university governance. Curiously, though, Bérubé urges us away from those byways—part of that "too simplistic," hairy-chested class analysis, I guess—and cautions against pitting "distinguished chairs against their teaching assistants." I confess this is something I just don't get: We have an institution—university tenure—that breeds a notoriously solidarity-resistant brand of occupational privilege, and out of deference to that institution's prerogatives, we craft a trade unionist strategy. Of course, it could be that the beneficiaries of such privilege are strenuously trying to pass their interests off under a cloud of vanguardist mystification. . . . Damn, there I go again. Where does one get counseling for this sort of thing?

One little-acknowledged piece of collateral damage from the culture wars is the way that their tendentiousness pretty much flattens most considerations of simple intellectual honesty. But even so, Bérubé's considerably less-than-close reading of my essay is rather stunning. He claims my piece opens by citing Russell Jacoby, when there is, in fact, a long opening epigraph by Thorstein Veblen; Jacoby doesn't put in his sinister appearance until the bottom of the third page. (But then, by his own admission, Bérubé appears to have read the whole thing back-to-front; perhaps this explains much of his outrage over my prose style.) I'm also excoriated for my "opportunistic tendency" to reprove the *Social Text* crowd for not writing on the Adelphi and Arizona International University cases "before they occurred." Well, the Adelphi crisis began in the fall of 1995, when the first reports of Adelphi President Peter Diamandopoulos's college-procured luxury condo became public. And the founding of the tenure- and union-free Arizona International University was announced in February 1996—after six years of widely reported public planning. The *Social Text* issue I criticized appeared in December 1996. In seeking to upend my argument that the academic vision of business and labor conditions at American universities tends to be as foreshortened as that famed Saul Steinberg cartoon of *The New Yorker*'s view of the world, Bérubé unwittingly proves my point.

Likewise, another of my piece's central points—that we see in academic labor discourse a persistent effort to transmute matters of class into matters of culture—receives, alas, abundant confirmation in Bérubé's hands. In fact, we see in Bérubé's various overheated asides a cultural reductionism that is indistinguishable from the person of Bérubé himself. I honestly don't know why it should matter that Bérubé appeared on picket lines as a toddler or that he grew up in a Shanker-hating "old labor house." In a profession that routinely decries the evils of essentialism, this display of quasi-genetic lefty street cred is an aporia indeed. (Though come to think of it, as a grade-schooler at a Seventies antiwar rally I was once struck on the head by a falling cardboard box. Does that count?)

But gaze across Bérubé's discursive landscape, and you see all manner of personalities dotting the horizon as sort of stand-up punching dolls, marking the contested turf of the culture wars. Hence the ritual plunging of me into the ranks of the Albert Shankers and the Pat Robertsons—and the frankly bizarre web of guilt-by-association he perceives emanating from the Venice study of Russell Jacoby (whose work, let the record show, I do indeed admire). In Bérubé's world, as in the discursive labors of so many acolytes of the New Left, all permissible debate flows from personal authenticity—and critique of any sort is suborned automatically to personal-cum-professional intrigue. (On the other hand, I'm grateful I got off comparatively lightly; in a recent *Nation* review of the culture wars tome *History on Trial*, Bérubé darkly hints that Elizabeth Fox-Genovese is a crypto-Aryan apologist for critiquing the history standards promulgated by an NEH task force in 1994.)

This rampant personalization of political argument intersects nicely with Bérubé's pronounced obsession with professional prestige. What seems to make Bérubé most apoplectic—enough so that he actually addresses me as "boy," a smirking juvenile afflicted with all manner of attention deficits—is that I'm nowhere to be found on the academic radar. Hell, I'm *not even a Russell Jacoby*, that tortured, semi-employed soul who lies awake counting the "general-interest lefty journals" that invite Bérubé's contributions. Next to Robin D.G. Kelly and Rick Wolff, I'm a mere poser and posturer. This feverish reckoning of positions by force of personal association is, indeed, the currency of argument itself: We are instructed to accept Bérubé's interpretations because another left academic—Jon Wiener in *Dissent*—says pretty much the same thing.

But where, oh where, would the personalization of political conflict be without the more legible and carnivalesque markers of the fashion system? In a self-dramatizing flourish almost too status-happy to be believed, there is Bérubé's endorsement of high fashion in the pursuit of academic renown, as reported in a recent issue of the *Chronicle of Higher Education*. Bérubé wowed last winter's MLA confab in Toronto, it seems, with what the *Chronicle* calls "an electric blue suit of 100 percent polyester"—and the smashing figure he cut with it is displayed, quite winsomely, in a four-color *Chronicle* photo. "It's an amazing color, and it never loses its crease!" this son of the picket line enthuses, after decrying the academy's low-end fashion standards: "Anything with some cut or color draws derision—and admiration—because the sartorial requirements of the business are so low." You know what? I think Bérubé may be onto something with this institutional culture of elitism, after all.

All right, all right—I know I'm being snide, in a manner entirely unbecoming of my station. As Bérubé says, there is much we agree on, and I don't want to go on reciting the long-familiar follies of the culture wars. I do, however, want to decamp from the cold Northeast for a luxury cruise. So, without further ado, here's a passage from the introduction to *Bad Subjects: Political Education for Everyday Life*, which Bérubé cowrote with Janet Lyons. It has critspeak, revolutionary praxis, and unwieldy metaphor to burn (the emphasis is also in the original):

> The curious thing about both political and aesthetic avant-gardes, though, is that they both subscribe to the ideology of alternative production: avant-garde work is subversive, is oppositional, *insofar as it circulates outside the system of exploitation and domination*, either because its point of origin is radically opposed to the system (for example, in the anarcho-syndicalist workers' collective) or because it works "underground," burrowing its corrosive way into the system from an external location that will be internal before the system knows what's hit it.

I'm thinking, I dunno, Antigua. And I'll be packing my electric blue beach robe.

The Guns of Santiago
Chronicle of My Death Postponed

MARC COOPER

8:30 A.M. Tuesday, September 11, 1973

THE rising Santiago sun and the blossoming jacaranda made the Chilean morning glorious. As I stood in the yard of my friend Melvin's suburban countryish house those twenty-five years ago, as I sucked the fragrant misty air into my lungs, I resolved I would, from that moment forward, make a change in my life. Quit smoking, cut back on drinking, get to bed before 3 A.M. and start rising earlier to be able to more frequently partake of these morning wonders. I had gotten up early because my Chilean residency visa expired that day and I needed to renew it—a process that could take hours.

For the past year I had been working as a translator for Chile's socialist president, Salvador Allende. Three years before, in September 1970, Allende had won a 36 percent plurality in a three-way presidential race; promising a "Chilean way to Socialism," Allende vowed profound but peaceful change. After all, Chile had a long tradition of parliamentary democracy and large, well-established left-wing political parties.

Allende kept to his pacifist promises, but his adversaries didn't. Even before he was inaugurated, a CIA-backed plot resulted in the kidnap and murder of army chief Rene Schneider. I arrived in Chile a few months later, expelled from the California university system by a certain Governor Reagan for my antiwar activism. Before long, I signed on as a translator for a large publishing company that Allende had nationalized. A year later I was asked if I would work as the president's translator. I was twenty-one. I was in awe.

It wasn't only the romance of revolution that lured me, but my reverence for Allende himself, a politician of absolute principle and the deepest sincerity. He was a gentleman revolutionary; I was fascinated by his formidable political skills, talents that even his most bitter enemies will acknowledge. But more striking still was the social process that took hold after his election. While the Sixties were dying out in America and Europe, in Chile they seemed to be reaching a stirring crescendo. Workers got organized, and students, shantytown dwellers, farm workers, women, and pensioners all followed suit. Politics were in command. One's party membership became the defining factor of one's personal identity. An entire society was reinventing itself.

Meanwhile, I was to help put together the English language version of *ChileInforma*, the government's monthly diplomatic newsletter. And from my office in the National Palace I was to translate Allende's speeches and writings into English for publication. The most attractive part of the job was those dozen or so meetings, usually late in the evening, when Allende would sit across a table from me and painstakingly correct and amend my work. We were not friends, of course: He was forty years older than me. But his manner was, as they say in Chilean Spanish, "correct"—a gracious, Old World patience.

But on the morning of September 11, 1973 my official status would give me little advantage in navigating Chile's Napoleonic bureaucracy. An early start was imperative.

But this was going to be difficult. The taxi companies, like many of the businesses owned by the Chilean ruling class, had joined a work stoppage led by the truck owners' association—a group floated with CIA dollars, we later discovered in congressional hearings. In daily entreaties, the country's owners pleaded openly with the armed forces to do away with the popularly elected Allende. Indeed, the entire country teetered on the brink of chaos and blood. As Allende carried out his reform program—nationalizing the copper mines and the telephone company, redistributing rural estates to sharecroppers, raising wages and giving unions a voice in national affairs, lowering rents and raising taxes on the rich—the right wing and eventually the center simply gave up on the idea of the rule of law. Chain-swinging thugs disrupted pro-government marches. Oil pipelines were dynamited. Industrial production was sabotaged. The wealthy hoarded food and other consumer goods and then loudly protested the resulting shortages.

Open military mutiny had broken out once already. Six weeks earlier, an army tank regiment allied with a neo-Nazi group had rolled out of its headquarters and shot up the Moneda Presidential Palace before loyal troops could smother the rebellion. The tension in Santiago had been crackling ever since. For many of us, it was no longer a question of whether a violent confrontation was coming: We only wondered if the army rank and file would follow their officers or remain loyal to the government— that is, provided the government even put up a fight.

Just a week previous to this morning, on September 4, the Chilean left held an enormous public gathering to commemorate the third anniversary of Allende's election. While Allende stood granite-faced on a balcony from the early afternoon till late into the night, more than a half-million Chilean workers and their families marched before him, voicing the nearly unanimous chant: "We want guns! We want guns!" It was a horrible, wrenching moment, one permanently seared into my memory. Yes, guns. But what guns? From where?

In the seven days that followed, the right only drew the noose tighter. Commerce and transportation ground to a halt. On the night of the tenth, my girlfriend and I had visited Melvin's house; stranded by the transportation stoppage, we had spent the night there. On the morning of the eleventh I phoned my friends at RadioTaxi 33, the revolutionary cab company, for a ride downtown.

After a forty-five minute wait on the corner I became concerned. I went back in the house to call the taxi again. But now the phone lines seemed permanently busy. I walked back to the corner and when the first freelance cab sped by I flagged it down. The driver, pale and harried, rolled down the window.

"Can you take me downtown?" I asked.

"Downtown?

"Yeah. To the immigration office," I answered.

With classic Chilean diplomacy the cabby said, "But, sir, there are problems downtown."

"Problems?"

"Yes, problems." He refused to be more specific. These were highly polarized times and you never knew who you were talking to. But a sinking in my gut told me the worst was upon us.

Mustering my own diplomatic skills, I asked: "Problems, you say? Problems with men in uniform you mean?"

"Yes, sir, problems with men in uniform," the cabby said. Then he took what he knew would be his last foray into freedom for some time and added: "Yes, the fucking fascists are overthrowing the government."

Everyone else in the house was still asleep. I switched on the massive Grundig radio and waited skittishly for the vacuum tubes to warm up. When the audio came alive I whooshed across the dial—virtually every station was playing the same military march. A stern-sounding announcer suddenly materialized: A military junta led by General Augusto Pinochet was seizing power. By order of the new authorities, he said, all radio stations were to immediately link up to the armed forces network or "they will be bombarded." Some more Prussian marches. And then another announcement. An ultimatum to President Allende. Either resign immediately or the Moneda Palace will also be bombarded. Another announcement told of a curfew "until further notice." Anyone found on the streets "will be shot on sight."

By 9:30 I had roused the others in the house. We sat dumbfounded in that chilled living room listening to the Communist Party station resist the order, urge workers to report to their work sites, and organize defense committees. But it was a futile gesture. Those of us who worked in the government knew the sad truth: that in spite of the right-wing chorus that Allende had formed a "parallel army," nothing of the kind existed. Allende had been scrupulous in his commitment to a constitu-

tional, legal, and peaceful vision of socialism. The only guns in the country, he vowed, would remain in the hands of the armed forces. Those who had profited from the constitutional system for 150 years were now smashing it beyond repair because it no longer served their immediate interests. The last man left standing in defense of the "bourgeois" constitution would be the socialist president, AK-47 in hand.

Miraculously, my first attempt to phone the office where I worked in the Moneda Palace went through. Over the sound of crackling gun fire, a secretary, Ximena, told me in tears that she and the others were about to flee the building. My next call was to the U.S. Embassy, on the fourteenth floor of an office building kittycorner to the Moneda. Why I called I don't remember very clearly. I had virtually no contact with them before. But I probably hoped that some provision was being made to provide safety for resident Americans. I figured it was only a matter of hours before I would be swept up into the military dragnet.

The embassy phone answered on the first ring. The accent on the line told me I was speaking with a Chilean employee, usually more American than the Americans. When I asked if the embassy had issued any special instructions, my respondent only laughed. "No special orders. Just stay off the streets." And then with another chuckle she added: "I'm looking out the window now with binoculars. Looks like Mr. Allende is finally going to get it." She hung up on me.

Within two hours, the Air Force had bombed the Socialist Radio Corporación and Radio Portales off the air. But Salvador Allende's metallic voice came live over Radio Magallanes. Via telephone, from inside the Moneda, with troops and tanks poised outside, with Hawker-Hunter jets arming their rockets in ready, Allende said:

> With my life I will pay for defending the principles dear to our nation. . . . History cannot be stopped by repression or violence. . . . Workers of my country: I will always be by your side, at least you will remember me as a man of dignity that was loyal to his country. You must know that, sooner rather than later, the grand avenues on which a free people walk will open and a better society will be at hand. . . . These are my last words.

It was a moment of devastating realization. The four of us sat in that living room listening and sobbing for I don't know how long. We had no access to any information except what the military broadcast over the radio. The phone lines were dead. We couldn't set foot out on the street. But everything I had learned over the previous two years told me the Chilean revolution had come to a dead end.

By two o'clock a cascade of military communiqués had come over the radio: That the Moneda had been bombed. That Allende was dead. That all political activity was banned. That the Allende gov-

ernment political parties were banned, the others "recessed." That the new junta was led by General Augusto Pinochet. That the citizenry should denounce all "suspicious foreigners."

As that first evening under military rule enveloped us I felt as if I were already in prison. I knew I would be a prime target: Allende's translator, an activist in the radical wing of the Socialist Party, and a foreigner at a moment when all foreigners were suspects. I cringed when I thought of my own apartment: a downtown high-rise located directly across the street from the new junta headquarters. Régis Debray, the French writer and radical who had spent time with Che Guevara in Bolivia, had lived in my building when Allende first came to power. Other units were rented to exiled guerrillas from Argentina and Uruguay. The building literally teemed with the international New Left. On my desk were all the copies of the work I had translated for Allende. In my top drawer was my passport and a visa to Cuba, where I was scheduled to accompany Allende. And to top it off, a popgun .22 revolver with two boxes of rounds. In short, once the troops broke into my apartment, there would be an APB out for a twenty-two-year-old American named Marc Cooper.

I remember that first night and the next day, Wednesday, as a blur. I know I didn't sleep well. I imagined Allende riddled and bloodied. I thought of the Moneda reduced to rubble by rockets and fire. I thought of the poor neigh-borhoods now surrounded and occupied by vengeful troops. I wondered about my friends; about the journalists, my co-workers. How many were already dead? How many would I ever see again? How long would it be before the troops came crashing through Melvin's door? I thought of the celebrations no doubt taking place that night in the creamy suburbs of Providencia and Las Condes. I winced at what I knew would be the wave of murder and torture that was about to wash over all of Chile. I wondered how the hell I was going to get out alive.

I remember getting up at four in the morning and shaving off my beard. I opened my wallet, took out my union card, my Socialist Party membership, my ID from the Moneda, and set them ablaze.

The next two days were marked by the sort of incipient madness that accompanies solitary confinement. We had little food in the house. Melvin, a thirty-year-old Bronx-born American, never told me why he was in Chile. I suspect he was ducking a drug possession charge. A fervent Allende supporter—and a fervent street-level trader—he made his living buying and selling on the black market. So we had on hand only a freezer full of Eskimo pies, several hundred pounds of onions, and a case of Pisco brandy. This odd diet, peppered with fear, drove me into a feverish, swirling retreat. I could barely talk to my Chilean girlfriend—now my wife—Patricia. I slept, paced, cried, ate ice cream, read Jim Thompson novels, and waited for either the curfew to lift or the door to come crashing down. But mostly we sat and listened to the radio. List after list of the wanted: Allende's cabinet ministers, party activists, union leaders, prominent and not-so-prominent exiles had their names read over the air and were ordered to surrender at the Ministry of Defense. How they were supposed to even step out on the curfew-swept streets and not get shot was never explained. As every reading began, I was sure my name would be next.

10 A.M. Friday, September 14

MELVIN and his girlfriend had drunk themselves into a stupor. So when the radio announced that the curfew would for the first time be lifted for five hours, Patricia and I decided we would have to leave Melvin's. She had to check on her family. I had to get my passport out of my apartment and figure a way to safety. Two weeks before the coup my former roommate, Carlos Luna, an exiled Argentine guerrilla, showed up at my apartment with a 9mm automatic. "The shit is coming," he said, pulling the pistol from his jacket. "When it does, I am getting into the Swedish Embassy even if I have to shoot my way in." But I had no such formidable weapon nor so much courage. The military had already announced that rings of troops were blocking off the European embassies. I wondered what had become of Carlos. Perhaps he, too, was dead by now.

During the break in the curfew, a deli owner who was a client of

Melvin's came to the house in his three-cylinder Citroneta. Well-connected to the military, I took his word at face value. "Cooper, you're fucked," he said matter-of-factly. "Your apartment has been raided and they're out looking for you." I asked him to drive me somewhere safe. He refused.

I began to panic. For the next four hours, during the window in the curfew, I would be able to move—but I had nowhere to go. My apartment had been trashed, I believed, my passport seized, my name on a wanted list, and the streets full of soldiers and checkpoints.

The phone was working again. And in what must have been the final moment of gross naiveté in my adult life, I thought again of the U.S. Embassy. I had an image in my head from Rossellini's *Open City*, of embassy staff cars rushing around the battle-littered streets, their white flags flapping. I am embarrassed now, twenty-five years later, to confess I thought that, given the mounting bloodshed in Chile, the American Embassy on that day would be sending cars out to pick up beleaguered stragglers like myself.

I was under absolutely no illusions, however, as to where the embassy stood politically. The Nixon-Kissinger regime had made clear its intention to do away with Allende and it was now three days deep into realizing that goal. But I was deluded enough to think that the U.S. government—perhaps out of humanitarian concern, perhaps merely to avoid the uncomfortable spectacle of American citizens mur-

dered by its new client dictator—would do something to protect us. I was very wrong.

At any rate, I called the U.S. Consulate. Explaining merely that I was an "American student," that I had done nothing wrong, but that the Chilean police had raided my apartment and seized my passport, I told Vice-Consul Tipton I needed help.

"Do you have a U.S. driver's license?" she asked me.

"Yes."

"Good," Ms. Tipton said. "Don't bother to come in today because we're about to close. But come in on Monday. Bring your license and ten dollars and we'll expedite you a new passport. Should take about a week, maybe ten days."

Stupefied, I argued with her. But to no avail. No special instructions to U.S. citizens were being offered. "Just stay away from shooting and obey the new authorities," Vice-Consul Tipton said. As far as the embassy was concerned my predicament was a simple case of a lost passport. Not that they didn't know the dangers posed by the coup, by the soldiers rounding up political rivals, by the indiscriminate executions that had already started. They had made a political calculation, and they were sticking by it, even if an occasional American had to die.

The embassy's stiff-arm made me desperate. I rummaged through my mental Rolodex and focused on a long shot. An American friend of mine, an Allendista, had told me some months before that a guy named Dennis Allred, who served as the U.S. Embassy's student affairs counselor, was actually a fine fellow. Allred, my friend told me, was some sort of closet Allende sympathizer and was taking secret delight in handing out U.S. scholarships to the most radical of Chilean students. True or not, it was good enough for me.

I phoned the embassy. No, I was told, Mr. Allred wasn't in. But, yes, being a fellow American, I could have his home phone number.

"Dennis, you don't know me," I told him after he answered his phone. "But I'm an American and I'm in trouble. I need. . . ."

"Okay," he said, cutting me short. "I don't care about the details. If you need a place to stay you're welcome here. Come now. I'm at 280 Merced." I thanked him and hung up. 280 Merced? That would put him right next door to the heavily guarded U.S. Consulate. Could I get past the troops?

Patricia and I hurriedly made a plan. She would catch a bus to her parents' home but first she would swing by the apartment and check its condition. She would call me later at Allred's. Meanwhile, I would have to walk the seven miles to Allred's house as I had no ID and buses were being boarded and checked by soldiers.

Melvin, who is six-foot-two, gave me a pair of clean pants. I am five-foot-three. I tucked the bottom of my pants up and inside and pinned them with safety pins. He gave me a fresh shirt and I rolled the sleeves up over my wrists. On top I had my black leather jacket.

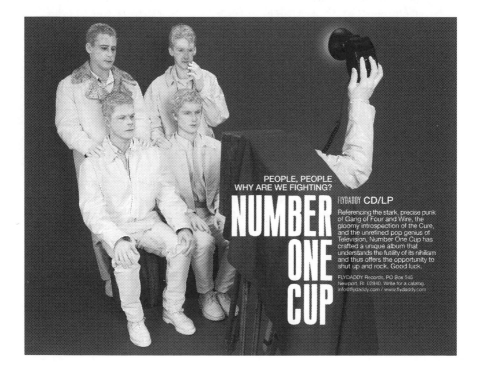

For three hours I trudged toward Allred's house, protected only by sunglasses, taking side streets and looking far ahead for any checkpoints. By four o'clock I was on the perimeter of the U.S. Consulate. Neighboring Forestal Park was an armed camp. Armored troop carriers bristled with machine guns. Troops had bivouacked in the park. In front of the consulate, a few steps from Dennis Allred's apartment, a company of soldiers lounged around on a tank.

I could hear my heart beating in my ears. I had no idea what I would tell the soldiers if they challenged me. I walked straight ahead, my eyes fixed on the door of Allred's building, my pace steady. Like passing through a time warp, I floated into the building uninterrupted. A big red-headed Bostonian, Allred greeted me alone in his luxury apartment. I was so pent-up I could hardly talk at first. And then I began to talk too much.

"I don't need to hear the details of your story. You can stay here as long as you have to," he said. He offered me a tumbler full of Old Grand-Dad, which I gulped down like water. The booze took the edge off, and I slumped back in the broad, padded mahogany chair. I called Patricia. I was relieved to hear that my apartment had *not* been raided. She got in, got my passport and a couple hundred dollars out, and tossed my .22 with its two boxes of ammo down the chute to the incinerator. She would come and visit me the next day when the curfew was again to be lifted for a short time.

Over a real meal that evening— salad and Kraft macaroni and cheese—Dennis Allred told me the good and the bad. "This apartment theoretically has diplomatic immunity, theoretically Chilean security cannot enter," he said. "On the other hand, the morning of the coup, the U.S. Embassy took my passport, locked it in a safe, sent me home, and told me they'd call me when I should come back into work. So I don't know how much protection we really have."

That night, as the saddest of Portuguese *fadas* played on Allred's stereo, drowning out the sporadic gunfire and the rumble of tanks, I slept soundly for the first time in almost one hundred hours.

6 P.M. *Sunday, September 16*

THE word was apparently out on Allred's generosity. Over the weekend the apartment had filled up with other hunted prey. A few had been beaten by troops who had broken down their doors. Others, like me, had nowhere to go. Others were there because I had contacted them. Allred had taken the courageous step of abandoning his direct-dial diplomatic phone to us—a luxury in a country where long distance calls were difficult to make in the best of times, and where the so-called "press calls" we were making now had to be cleared by a military censor. With Allred's diplomatic phone we skipped over all the obstacles. We set up a mini-information clearinghouse in his study, calling around the city to check on the safety of friends and co-workers. We painstakingly cobbled together lists of those who were safe, those who had been arrested, and those who were simply missing. Having compiled the information from a mix of sources—friends, reporters, diplomats, health workers, UN functionaries—we were able to skirt Chilean censorship and pass it along directly to family, media, and human rights groups in the United States.

A few friends that came by Allred's house told tales of serious resistance, of a rallying of Allende forces, of guns that were on their way, of former General Carlos Prats, who had been forced from office a few weeks before the coup by the right, who was now said to be pulling together a people's army. These rumors all sounded wonderful. And we knew they were all false. The Chilean army, the business elite, and the CIA had won their victory early that first morning when the soldiers obeyed their officers and when Allende perished inside the Moneda. Now they were just mopping up the rest of us.

And there was still no way out of Chile. The airports were closed. The embassies sealed. Any foreigner on the street was a suspect automatically. Who knew whose names were on the myriad arrest and shoot-on-sight lists.

A friend of mine, a Mexican reporter, called me from his country's embassy. Would I be interested in getting on a list that the Mexican Embassy was putting together to be evacuated? Absolutely. I gave him the names of three or four other desperate friends. He told me to sit tight and wait, that word of the flight out could come at any time. I had no choice but to comply.

Noon, Monday, September 17

WORD came that some Americans were missing, our friend Charlie Harmon among them. We would see Harmon next a decade later as a celluloid ghost conjured up in the Costa-Gavras film *Missing*— an innocent who had been seized, shot, and dumped by Chilean troops. But that morning we only knew Charlie was missing. We were worried about him, worried about all of us. One young American professor rallied us in Allred's living room and we went as a group next door to speak to the U.S. consul.

Enough was enough, we shouted. We wanted the U.S. Embassy to do what every other diplomatic delegation was doing in Chile—protecting its own citizens from a rampaging, barbarous military. The consul stood in the hall, blocking access to his office. Again he ran through the party line: He would look into Harmon's case, but there was nothing else to be done. The State Department had still issued no special instructions for Americans in Chile. "I recommend you just be careful," the consul said. And then he had the nerve to look us in the eye and come up with a straight-out lie: "The armed forces are restoring order, but there's still a danger of scattered left-wing snipers. Be careful." And with that he shooed us out of the consulate.

What we should have done, of course, was just sit down on the bastard's floor. But instead we slumped back to Allred's apartment, which soon shook with an enormous thud. Then another. From the second-floor balcony we could see two tanks squatting comfortably in the park, lobbing artillery rounds across the river into the fine arts campus of the University of Chile. That's how the armed forces were restoring order.

8 P.M. Tuesday, September 18

ONE week since the coup and the call finally came through from the Mexicans. Thanks to the Mexican government I was to be on a flight the next morning organized by the UN High Commissioner for Refugees. Apart from a special military plane that carried Allende's widow to Mexico, this would be the first flight allowed out of Chile. There was a catch, of course. I had to be at the distant Sheraton Hotel the next morning at 7:30 sharp. But curfew didn't lift till 7. It was going to be tight. Nor could I get word to Patricia to meet me to say goodbye. She used a neighbor's phone and if I called her now, at night, she would have to defy the curfew.

Emotionally, this was the worst it got. I was ecstatic at the thought I might get out the next day, but terrified that something might go wrong. And deeply depressed at the same time, with a bad case of survivor's guilt. My only prospect for happiness was to flee the slaughterhouse of my friends.

7 A.M. Wednesday, September 19

THE moment the curfew lifted I called Patricia and asked her to do what she could to meet me at the Sheraton. I hugged Allred goodbye. With only my passport, two hundred dollars in cash, and the borrowed clothes on my back I walked past the encampment of soldiers outside Allred's door. On the corner, a daring taxi driver stood ready for the post-curfew fares. When we arrived at the Sheraton, I reached into my pocket to pay. The cabby turned around and commenced one more of those skillfully coded dialogues.

"Are you a foreigner?" he asked.

"Yes, an American."

"Have you been living in Chile?" he asked, probably noting my accent.

"Yes, for nearly three years."

"Are you leaving today?"

"Yes. I am leaving."

"Then there will be no charge," the cabby said. "I want your thoughts about your last moments in Chile to be positive ones."

Operating on an emotional hairtrigger, I couldn't answer through my tears. I only nodded.

Inside the Sheraton lobby I was met by UN and Mexican officials. There was to be a motley mix of about fifty of us on the flight. Few of us knew each other. There were some Spanish clergy, some Mexican teachers, an American researcher black and blue from a beating, and a Texas high school swim team that had the bad luck of passing through Santiago on the wrong day. Because Americans were on the flight manifest,

American consular officials had showed up as well, with clipboards in hand. We refused to talk to them.

Just before we boarded the bus to the airport, Patricia arrived for a short goodbye. Under heavy military escort we were taken to the Cerrillos military air base. After the junta's new immigration officers raised a perfunctory challenge or two to the validity of our UN-secured safe-conduct passes we were herded onto a corporate 737 owned by LADECO, one of the copper companies nationalized by Allende.

There was an eerie silence through takeoff. No one was sure of anyone else on the plane. Then, a half-hour into the flight, a crackling voice came over the intercom.

"Ladies and gentlemen," the captain said crisply. "We have just entered Argentine air space."

The plane erupted in yelps of joy and applause. In seconds we were all on our feet embracing each other, even the Texas swim team. The Kool-Aid and baloney sandwiches served aboard remains the best airplane meal I've ever had.

We were greeted in Buenos Aires as heroes. That night we marched with 100,000 Argentines to protest the Chilean military dictatorship.

Patricia called me the next week to tell me that on September 22, she went by my apartment to find the front door blown off its hinges, the entire place sacked by soldiers.

She came to the States two months later and we have been married ever since.

Dennis Allred resigned from the U.S. Foreign Service.

Ten years later, passing through Sweden, I found my old guerrilla roommate Carlos Luna running an import-export business with Cuba.

During the ensuing seventeen years of Pinochet's dictatorship, more than three thousand civilians were murdered by the government while more than a thousand were "disappeared." One hundred thousand Chileans passed through jails where torture was routine, and more than twice that number sought asylum abroad. Allende's foreign minister, Orlando Letelier, was killed in Washington, D.C., by a car bomb planted by Chilean secret police. Pinochet's predecessor, General Prats, was blown apart by a similar bomb in Buenos Aires. American economists invited to Chile by Pinochet imposed a radical free-market model on the country, eventually submerging a third of its population into abject poverty. As late as 1997 *The New York Times* was still celebrating Pinochet's takeover as a "coup that began Chile's transformation from a backwater banana republic to the economic star of South America." The weak civilian government that took over in 1990 has not prosecuted Pinochet's torturers or murderers. Today retired General Pinochet sits as senator-for-life in the Chilean Congress.

During his final speech on Radio Magallanes Salvador Allende promised us that one day there would be a "moral punishment" for the crime and treason that killed him and his Chile. We are still waiting.